Dare to collect them all!

THE MIDNIGHT LIBRARY

End Game

Nick Shadow

Hodder
Children's
Books

A division of Hodder Headline Limited

Special thanks to Ben Jeapes

Text copyright © 2005 Working Partners Limited
Illustrations copyright © 2005 David McDougall
Created by Working Partners Limited, London W6 0QT

First published in Great Britain in 2005
by Hodder Children's Books

3

A Catalogue record for this book is available from
the British Library

ISBN-10: 0 340 89407 5
ISBN-13: 9780340894071

Typeset in Weiss Antiqua by Avon DataSet Ltd,
Bidford-on-Avon, Warwickshire

Printed and bound in Great Britain by
Clays Ltd, St Ives plc

The paper and board used in this paperback by
Hodder Children's Books are natural recyclable products
made from wood grown in sustainable forests. The manufacturing
processes conform to the environmental regulations
of the country of origin.

Hodder Children's Books
a division of Hodder Headline Limited
338 Euston Road
London NW1 3BH

Welcome, reader.

My name is Nick Shadow,
curator of that secret
institution:

The Midnight Library

Where is the Midnight Library, you ask?
Why have you never heard of it?
For the sake of your own safety, these questions are better left
unanswered. However ... so long as you promise not to reveal
where you heard the following (no matter who or *what*
demands it of you), I will reveal what I
keep here in the ancient vaults.
After many years of searching,
I have gathered the most terrifying
collection of stories known to
man. They will chill you to
your very core, and make
flesh creep on your young,
brittle bones. Perhaps you should
summon up the courage and turn the
page. After all, what's the worst that
could happen ... ?

M L

The Midnight Library: Volume III

Stories by Ben Jeapes

CONTENTS

END GAME

The inside of the car was soundproofed, and a glass partition cut off the front seats from the back. The only sound in the rear was Simon's game: the *bleep-bleep-bleep* as he worked the controls, the triumphant tinny fanfare as another dragon bit the dust. He didn't hear the crackle of wheels on gravel as the car swept up the drive to the house. His eyes were fixed on the small LCD screen of the handheld PC. He had been battling at this game for so long, but if he remembered the cheat hint on the website – the paladin must get off his horse *before* he walks through the gate, so that the dragon misses him when it swoops down – but do it too soon and the bridge crumbles and you fall to your death, so it has to be *just right*.

The chauffeur opened the door and a blast of cold air hit him on the side of the face.

'We're home, Master Simon,' the man said.

Simon Down glared at him, then at the screen, just as the paladin's headless body toppled to the ground. He had been distracted at exactly the wrong moment. The dragon swooped up into the air, the head clutched between its claws and dripping a digital trail of red blobs.

'You're fired!' Simon shouted.

'If you say so, Master Simon,' the man replied. 'Dinner will be at seven.'

Of course, Simon thought as he slouched into the house, he didn't really have the authority to fire anyone. You couldn't do that when you were twelve. But it was a nice thought, being able to control the outside world as well as he could control the one in his computers.

He paused at the front door, and twisted round to look back. The house was set high above the treeline and overlooked the entire town. Down there, Simon thought, there were other people. He bit his lip. His schoolmates were down there. People with lives. People with each other.

It was a lonely thought, but Simon had got good at turning the lonely thoughts against themselves. Yes, they had each other, he told himself, but they lived their lives crammed together. Constantly rubbing shoulders. Constantly in each other's way.

But up here he was free, above them all, looking down on them all.

He had tried inviting some of them back to his place, once. Mum had suggested it. She had probably read it in a book on child development:

'encourage your child to make friends'. But none of them had come, even though Simon had described the huge television set, his vast library of games and DVDs. He had even exaggerated a teeny bit – he didn't *really* have a den with flatscreen televisions on every wall showing a dozen different channels all at once. But no, none of them had been interested.

Well, let them stay away, he decided, as he turned back to the house. Simon wouldn't let himself envy them. He had something that was better than anything they had. Something that was, in every sense, better than reality.

Hello SIMON and welcome to <u>betterthanrealitygames.</u>
<u>world</u> [If you're not SIMON then click here]

The words flashed on to the screen as Simon loaded the browser and settled down in front of his computer. He had set <u>betterthanrealitygames.world</u> as his home page, and the house had the fastest broadband connection you could get. He just had to turn the computer on, and there it was.

The glow of the monitor was the only light in Simon's room. The bright reds and greens and yellows washed across his face and he smiled. The site was more reliable than any friend, warm and inviting and always there for him.

It had been a typical evening: homework, play games, eat, play more games. All supervised by the butler, Templeton, and Mrs Solomon, the housekeeper. Dad was still at the bank, and Mum was out doing her charity work. Then, at 9.30 sharp, bedtime. The servants wouldn't fuss if he stayed up, but his parents might if they happened to come home. They'd remember something they had once heard about bedtimes. Like they were good parents, or something.

But betterthanrealitygames.world was how Simon always ended his day. These games were definitely better than reality – better than anything else in his life, in fact. Games that made you think; games you couldn't just walk through. Games that were never the same twice.

As it always did, his mouse cursor hung over the link for 'custom-made games'. He had gone there once before, but one look at the prices had changed his mind. If only there were a free sample or demo – but no, once you got past the prices, you had to enter your card details. He didn't *have* a credit card, and he knew from experience there would be hell to pay if he entered Mum's or Dad's. That was one definite way of getting their attention, but it had drawbacks, like having his PC taken away for a week.

He sighed, and there was a knock at the door. It opened a crack and a woman's head poked round it. She had long, brown hair and wide-spaced, hazel eyes, just like Simon.

Simon jumped up. 'Mum!'

'Hello, darling. Still up?' Mrs Down didn't come into the room. 'I haven't seen much of you lately, have I? Go to bed now, and we'll have a good natter in the morning. Goodnight!'

The door closed before Simon could get a word in edgeways.

He turned back to the computer and logged off. 'A good natter in the morning,' he muttered to himself. Sure! Except that by the time he was up, she'd have some new emergency to deal with, and she'd have already left for the office. Her charity work looked after crises all around the world. Anything from distressed dolphins to Guatemalan orphans. Anything that wasn't him.

He switched the monitor off and the room was left in darkness.

Something was shining through Simon's eyelids. He pried them open and peered sleepily across the room. The monitor was on again, and the familiar bright colours of betterthanrealitygames.world were splashed around the room. Simon frowned. He was sure he had turned it off.

He curled up into a ball and pulled the duvet over his head. Somehow the light still got in, and he couldn't get back to sleep. He threw the cover back angrily. He would have to turn the thing off properly, and this time pull the plug to make sure.

But when he approached the computer, what he saw wasn't the usual welcome screen.

Hello SIMON. As one of our most valued customers we want to offer you a FREE CUSTOM-MADE GAME. Just fill in the boxes below and your FREE CUSTOM-MADE GAME will be posted direct to you.

'Free, huh?' Simon muttered. One thing he had learned a long time ago was that no successful company ever gave you something that was *really* free. But he would play along until he found what the catch was, then pull out.

So he sat down and placed his hand on the mouse.

First there was all the demographic guff. Age, gender, occupation – in other words, stuff that would go straight to the marketing department so that they could spam him for ever. He declared himself to be an eighty-year-old widow, employed as a brain surgeon, on a million pounds a year.

Then came the more important items.

YOUR GAME:
Would you like your game to be tame or dangerous?

Oh, please, Simon thought. He ticked 'dangerous' without even thinking about it.

Would you like your game to be set in your home town,
a generic town or a fantasy world?

The cursor hovered over 'fantasy world'. Set a game in his town? Yeah, right! Simon snorted. His town was . . . but, now he came to think of it, his town was *exactly* the kind of place that could do with a game being set there to liven it up a bit. So he clicked the 'home town' tab.

Would you like your game to be reality-based, or as real as life?

Simon frowned. What was the difference? Then he thought of those tedious arcade games where you control a skateboarder zooming for ever around a fantasy arena, or an unseen gunman blasting away at crooks and aliens in an endless maze. Those were reality-based, and you soon got the hang of them, once you realized they were all basically the same thing, over and over. Whereas, if anything could be said for real life, it was that each day could be completely different from the one before. So Simon moved the cursor over 'real life' and clicked.

He woke with a gasp. Sunlight was streaming through the curtains and birds sang outside. The blank screen of the computer stared impassively at him from across the room.

He frowned at it. Blank screen? He had turned it

off before going to bed, but hadn't it come on again, and hadn't he . . . ?

He shook his head to clear it. *Sure, Simon! Your computer offered you a free game! Get real.*

And then he looked at the bedside clock, and leaped out of bed with a yell. He had overslept by nearly an hour!

Simon showered, dressed and threw books in his bag at warp speed. He would have to skip breakfast. The car would take him to school at River Park, but it was as unforgiving as the school bus. It would leave square on the hour, whether he was ready or not – as well as taking Simon to school, it also had to collect his dad from his daily breakfast meeting. If Simon wasn't in it when it left, he would be in big trouble.

But there was one ritual which he had to go through, however late he was. He switched the computer on to check for messages.

Hello SIMON. Your custom game has been posted.

Simon recoiled. So he really had been offered a free game last night! Strange how he didn't remember going to bed again, though. But there was no time to think about it properly. He could hear the car drawing up on the drive. He ran out of the room, leaving it untidy and the bed unmade. The servants would set everything straight while he was gone.

When he came home that evening, the duvet cover was freshly washed and ironed. And lying on it was a brown paper parcel.

Simon put his schoolbag down and picked the parcel up. He turned it over in his hands. It was small and square, the size and weight of a DVD box. His name and address were printed in neat, handwritten capitals. There was no return address, and no postage either. Who was hand-delivering packages to him? he wondered.

He went out on to the landing. Templeton was crossing the hall and Simon called down to him.

'When did this arrive?'

The butler looked up in surprise. 'When did what arrive, Master Simon?'

Simon held the package up. 'This. For me.'

Templeton raised his eyebrows. 'You had no deliveries that I was aware of, Master Simon.'

Simon felt the first stab of suspicion. He would have sworn that Templeton had a certificate guaranteeing his lack of a sense of humour. Could the butler be winding him up?

'Did anyone go into my room today?' he asked.

'The housekeeper made your bed, Master Simon,' Templeton answered. 'But otherwise no, no one.'

Simon went back into his room and looked at the package. It couldn't have just appeared, could it? Someone *must* have left it.

Could someone have got up here without being noticed by the staff? Or was it just the housekeeper, playing her own little game?

Hey, get a grip! he told himself. There was no point getting paranoid. What was undeniable was that this package was here, right now.

He pulled the paper off and held up a DVD ROM in a plastic case. There was no label on the case or the disc – just the word 'Simon' written in black, indelible marker. Would the housekeeper be leaving him DVDs?

It took half a second to decide that no, she wouldn't. She had to ask advice on setting the video – she wasn't going to be burning discs in her spare time. Heart pounding, Simon switched the computer on and slid the DVD ROM into the tray.

The drive whirred into action and the screen cleared. A message flashed up in white lettering on a black background. It looked like the text on a really old, steam-driven DOS computer.

Welcome to your game, Simon.

So far, so sucky. He had seen better graphics on an eighties arcade-imitation game. The message was just basic computer text scrolling across the screen.

The welcome message scrolled up and was replaced by something slightly longer.

You control the actions of a dangerous criminal. The object of the game is to cause as much devastation as possible to the town.

Then came a description of how to use the controls, which he could have figured out in his sleep. It looked as basic as the first screen. Simon yawned as he picked up the joypad that was plugged into the back of his PC.

And then the screen cleared, and he sat bolt upright as reality seemed to pour into the room through the screen.

'Wow!' he breathed. He was looking down the local high street in town. It was like there was a camera there, piping real-time images straight to his PC. It wasn't jerky like a webcam, nor black and white like CCTV. His screen was filled with full colour, high-resolution pictures. His viewpoint seemed to be from about five metres up in the air, looking down and along the street.

It was the end-of-day rush hour. The road was thick with traffic, and the pavements were crowded. The sounds that filled his room were the sounds of the high street in late afternoon.

The only thing that told him it wasn't a livecam was the man standing in the middle of the road with his back to Simon. He just stood there, ignoring the traffic that crawled by on either side. He wore dirty old trainers, well-worn jeans and a T-shirt. You couldn't see his face, just the back of his close-cropped head. Looking at his broad shoulders and thick arms, he was the kind of guy Simon might think about crossing the road to avoid.

Simon nudged his joypad and the man moved forward a few paces. Left, and the man turned left. The whole scene shifted with him, so that the man kept his back to the screen. Now he was facing the shops.

No way, Simon thought, *no* way *can they have*

digitized the whole town in just a few hours! Because that was when he had placed his order, just a few hours ago. Did they have templates arranged for different towns? Or at least, all the towns in their customer database? But there, on screen, just to the left, was the church with scaffolding up the front. Simon drove past it every day on the way to school, and he knew the scaffolding had only gone up two days ago. They must have updated their database pretty fast. Maybe it was all tied in to some kind of satellite feed.

Whatever it was, he decided that he was going to test this simulation to the limit. They went to such efforts to make this seem completely real, it was his duty to try to break it. He set the man running at an easy, gentle lope along the pavement. People quickly got out of his way on either side. Sometimes they looked like people Simon knew -- the school librarian, someone who worked for his dad -- but then they were gone from view as the man ran on.

Using the joypad, Simon turned the man left off the high street and tried the park, the river, then a roundabout route back to the town centre. The man responded instantly to his every command, and there wasn't the slightest hint of a break between scenes. It was as if everything was really happening down there in the town.

The man came to a junction, and Simon took his hands off the joypad. He had tried sending the man randomly around the town; maybe he should start some kind of strategy. But what? On screen, the man had obediently stopped and was waiting for his next command.

Suddenly a message popped up in a box. It was the same old font, black on a grey background.

Remember, BRAINIAC, you are controlling a DANGEROUS CRIMINAL. So do something DANGEROUS.

'Well, excuse me for living,' Simon said. 'Got any

suggestions ... whoa!' As if in reply, another message had appeared.

Why not BREAK IN somewhere? You can choose:
- *the hospital*
- *the gasworks*
- *the bakery*

'The *bakery*?' Simon said scornfully. 'Sure, all dangerous criminals break into the *bakery*.'

But he selected the bakery anyway, because he wanted to test the game with the least obvious choice. And while he had nothing against the hospital (he might be ill one day) or the gasworks (he had to stay warm), the owner of the bakery in Bruton Street, two roads away from Simon's school, was another matter. The man was permanently grouchy and seemed to have a personal grudge against all the town's young people. *This*, Simon thought, *could be interesting*.

As soon as he made his choice, the man started to run back through the town.

'Hey, come on!' Simon protested. He had assumed that selecting the bakery option would take the man straight there, like jumping to another scene. But the downside of this game was that everything seemed to happen in real time, which meant that moving more than a short distance seemed to take forever. He pressed down hard on the joypad but the man kept running at the same pace. Simon had already got used to controlling the man's every move and it was a strange feeling, having to sit back and watch him.

The man turned into the shopping centre and jogged through it, stopping outside the bakery window. And there he stood, not moving. His hands hung by his sides and he stared through the plate glass at the racks of buns and cakes. His back was still turned to Simon, and his reflection in the glass was too dark for Simon to pick out any features.

'Hello?' Simon called out. 'Hell*oo*? Going anywhere?'

Still the man just stood, until Simon

experimentally prodded the joypad and he took a couple of steps.

'Yes!' Simon said in satisfaction. The man was back under control. Simon made him walk into the shop and look around. There were shelves full of loaves of bread, cakes, buns, cookies, and a glass-topped counter with the cash till on it. It was exactly as it always looked in real life.

'This is so wicked,' Simon murmured. He had thought that maybe the game's makers got their designs for the town from satellite images, but what satellite could look into a shop?

The owner of the bakery was behind the counter. He was middle aged, dark haired and plump, with a permanently sour expression. Like the inside of the shop, he looked just like the real thing.

'Can I help you?' the baker asked. Simon's speakers were good enough to make it sound like the man was in the room with him. It was even the same tone of voice he always used, suggesting he was only pretending to like the customer.

'Yeah, I'm going to smash the place up,' Simon said cheerfully to the screen. 'But first I'll take all your money, 'cos I'm a dangerous criminal.' He studied the buttons on the joypad. Was there anything to make the man talk? Apparently not. He assumed the man couldn't speak, so he just had him walk around the end of the counter towards the till.

'Hey!' The baker stepped forward and prodded the man in the chest. 'Back off!'

Simon hadn't yet made the man do anything apart from run. How could he fight back? On an impulse he pressed the red button on the joypad – the button he would press if this was a war game and he wanted to fire something. The man on the screen put his hand on the baker's chest and shoved, hard. The baker staggered back and smashed into a glass cabinet, the nerve-scraping sound of shattering glass reproduced perfectly by the computer's speakers. He cowered in the shards on the floor, staring up at his attacker with a terrified expression.

The man just stood there and looked back,

because Simon had forgotten to enter any more commands. He was gazing at the screen in stunned disbelief.

'Wow!' he whispered. He was used to combat games, games where improbable superhuman heroes could fling each other around like pillows. But there had been something *real* about this. The way the man had braced himself, the strength of his shove, it looked genuine, like one real flesh-and-blood human had just assaulted another.

Simon came back to himself with a shudder. *Hey, get a grip*, he told himself. However good the images were, they were all just bytes in a memory card. Nothing more. And he had unfinished business here.

Simon made his man turn towards the till, which opened with a *ka-ching*. He emptied the cash out into his pockets. Just before he turned the man to leave, a note popped up on the screen.

Want to cause some more damage? Remember — this is a
DANGEROUS CRIMINAL.

More damage? Why not! Simon thought. After all, it was only a game.

The man was standing next to some shelves. Simon pressed the red button again and the man grabbed the shelves, then heaved. Baked goods cascaded across the floor in clouds of flour. With a little further experimentation, Simon found that pressing the red button was enough to set the man into 'wreck' mode. If he was standing next to the baker, he hit him; if he was standing next to something breakable, he broke it.

Simon worked his way around the shop, smashing more shelves, kicking in the glass counter, pulling down the light fittings. Then he noticed a door behind the counter. Using the joypad, he steered the man over and wrenched it open. It led into a tile-lined room, lit by fluorescent striplights. Along one wall was a large, stainless steel baker's oven. The door in the front was metal and glass, and a row of dials and knobs ran along the top. A small message popped up in the top right-hand corner of the screen:

Move cursor over items to get values.

Simon slid the cursor over the oven.

Baking oven. Six months old. Retail value: £5000

Wow, it cost almost as much as his dad's TV!

You can cause some REAL damage in here, Simon!

Simon pressed the red button again, but this time the man just stood there.

Use the chair for maximum damage.

Chair? Simon made the man look around the room. There was a steel-framed chair in one corner, so he moved the man over to it. More experimenting showed that the green button made the man pick it up. Then it was back to the red button. The man hefted the chair up in both hands and swung it down hard against the oven. The speakers rattled with an ear-wrenching, metallic boom. On screen, the oven's dials shattered and some of the knobs snapped off. Simon smashed at it again and again, until the chair was just a pile of bent tubing and the oven was dented and battered like it had been in a train crash.

Shaking and breathing hard as if he was doing the wrecking himself, Simon sent the man into the next room. The baker obviously used this one as an office. The man overturned the desk and kicked the filing cabinets again and again, leaving satisfying, trainer-shaped dents in each drawer. There was a computer on the desk, so he picked that up and smashed it on the tile floor, and turned the desk over. Finally he flung the chair through the window.

Dimly, Simon could hear a police siren. He realized it was coming from the computer.

Cops coming. Better scram. You have:
- *Taken £788*

- *Caused £7093 pounds' worth of damage*

Your score is **7881**

Do you want to:
- *spend the money?*
- *hide the money?*

Simon thought. *What could you spend £788 on?* Not much, compared to what he already had in his bedroom. No, he would save up and buy something totally awesome. If there was some sort of virtual shop on this game, maybe he could buy the man some body armour or a weapon. Simon decided that he would wait. So he selected 'hide the money'.

Immediately, the man began to run again, out of the shop's back exit. He seemed to know exactly where he was going to hide the money. Like before, now he had a destination in mind there was no controlling him. Except that Simon didn't know where the destination was. What if he was going to hide his winnings in a useless place? There was no way this guy could know his town better than him. Simon shouted angrily and thumped the joypad. But the man kept running and Simon could only watch, frustrated.

On the screen the man was heading down the main road away from the town centre. Simon wondered where he was going. Did the man have a secret base or a hideout?

The man kept running. Simon twiddled his thumbs and mentally composed the feedback he wanted to leave at <u>betterthanrealitygames.world</u>. *The graphics are amazing, the action is incredibly real but the real-time element SUCKS!*

The man had reached the industrial estate on the edge of town, and was showing no signs of stopping. It seemed the game designer had decided that hiding the money meant leaving town altogether. On the screen, the road in front of the man started to curve up. Simon knew that route all too well. It was the road he took every day, to and from school. If he could make the man stop and turn round, there would be the whole of town spread out below him. But the man kept going, leaving the town further and further behind. Did the game's map of town extend all the way to the top of the hill? Was there a digitized mansion at the top with a tiny little Simon sitting in an upstairs room in front of an even tinier computer?

But after the fields, between the town and the top of the hill, were the woods. Once the forest had covered the whole hill. Now it was just a strip of trees near the top, a barrier that cut Simon's house off from the rest of town. The man entered the woods and for the first time, he turned off the road. Simon had another chance to marvel at the game's graphics, the way the setting sun beamed golden fans of light down through the branches.

About one hundred metres into the woods, the man stopped in front of an oak tree with initials carved into the bark. Briefly, Simon wondered who JV and ZD had been. The man kneeled down to clear a space in the moss between two roots and put the money into it. Then he covered it up again with moss and left a pine cone on top as a marker.

Simon glanced at the clock. He jumped. It was half past eight – he had been playing this game for the last four hours! Most of which, he supposed, had been watching the man run around town in real time. He was hungry – the house staff must have called him for dinner, but he hadn't heard – and his eyes were dry and aching.

He looked back at the game and bit his lip. He didn't want to leave it now, when he was just getting the hang of it. Problem was, if he sent the man back to town then he would have to sit through another hour of the guy running down the hill.

The screen was growing dark to match the time of day. Simon pressed some more controls to see if there was any kind of night vision facility. Apparently not.

The game made his mind up for him. The

man walked back to the road, then turned downhill to head back to town. A message flashed up on screen.

That's all for today, Simon. Hope it whetted your appetite.
See you tomorrow.

The screen went blank and the disc ejected itself, with a whir of gears.

'Wow,' Simon breathed.

He slowly removed the disc from its tray and returned it to its case. Then he switched the PC off. This game had some glitches, but at the same time it was the coolest thing he had ever seen. Ever.

Someone slammed into Simon, knocking the breath out of him. He staggered against the wall.

'Hey, mind where you're going, Down!'

Reality came flooding back in.

For most of the morning, Simon had been

distracted, thinking about the game. Now he was brought back to his surroundings with a jolt. He was at school, walking down the main corridor between lessons. It was a heaving mass of school uniforms and noisy chatter, caught in the brief break between lessons. But even though it was rammed with students going in every direction, most of the people using it managed not to walk into each other.

Apart from Mat Frost – tall, fair haired, good looking and a boy that Simon detested. Normally he was good at looking out for Mat, but today he had been too caught up with thoughts of the game, and what he would do with it tonight.

The two boys backed away from each other – Simon slowly and carefully, Mat with a slouch. Mat grinned and held Simon's gaze just long enough to make him look away. Simon turned to his locker and fumbled for his key, trying to look like that was what he had planned all the time. He knew from experience that if Mat Frost decided to have it in for him, the rest of the day could be unbearable.

But Mat was distracted by a cry from down the hall.

'Hey, Frost! Coming to the shops at breaktime?' It was Mat's best friend, Tom Mansbridge.

'You're kidding!' Mat said. 'Haven't you heard? There's police lines everywhere.'

'You what?'

Simon was still struggling with his locker key, but he couldn't help hearing. Half the school couldn't help hearing. He paused and listened.

'Major break-in yesterday at the bakery! Guy got really badly beaten up,' said Mat.

'No way!' replied Tom.

'Yeah, they emptied the till and smashed the place up, guy needed stitches . . .'

A small crowd was gathering to discuss the attack, and to his surprise, Simon felt his feet carrying him over. He stood on the fringes of the crowd. No one seemed to mind. He moved a little closer. A couple of the kids moved aside for him without taking their attention off Mat.

One of the younger boys – tubby, slightly spotty, just the type Mat would consider fair game – piped up. 'I really hope they get that guy!' he blurted. 'It's not right.'

Mat just looked at him. No sarcastic comment, no snide insult. 'Yeah,' he agreed. 'It's not right.'

That did it. If that kid could be accepted, Simon decided, so could he. He knew the whole bakery thing had to be one massive coincidence, but wouldn't they sit up and take notice if they knew what he had been playing last night!

He laughed a little too loudly, trying to make a joke. 'Yeah, that's the last time he tries to short-change me!'

It was like pricking a bubble. The mood in the crowd vanished, and several hostile stares turned on him. His face started to blaze.

Mat stared at him with contempt. 'Another of your fantasies, Down?' Most of the other boys started to drift off and Mat turned away from Simon to face Tom. 'Meet you at the lake after school, yeah? See if we can get some guys together.'

'Sure, Frosty. Sounds good.'

Simon made one last effort. 'Yeah. Um, see you there.'

Mat turned back to him. 'Sorry, Down. The lake's a nerd-free zone.' He and Tom laughed as they walked off down the corridor, leaving Simon standing on his own, with his fists clenched at his sides.

Somehow, Simon got through the rest of the day. Mat Frost was never far from his mind. He had been *that close* to being part of the crowd. He had something at home that could wipe the floor with Mat's popularity. If he could just find a way to let people know, then *he* would be popular. People would want to hang out with him.

Tall Mat. Good-looking Mat. Popular Mat. Mat who would be nothing without his car dealer dad.

Frost Senior owned a very upmarket dealership – expensive sports cars that would set you back a bank manager's salary or more. Mat was always talking about the flash models his dad got to test, usually with Mat in the passenger seat.

And what use are flash cars to school kids? Simon thought bitterly. None of us can drive! But everyone can play computer games, watch movies – all the things they could do in spades if they bothered to hang around with him.

The end-of-school bell that Friday afternoon was like a prison door opening. The playground was packed with kids milling around, waiting for pick-ups or the bus, or wheeling their bikes round from the racks behind the sports hall. As usual, the car was waiting for Simon, directly outside the gate. He pulled the door closed, and it cut off nearly all the noise outside; he pulled out his GameBoy and switched it on. The car pulled away.

'Good day at school, Master Simon?' the chauffeur asked without looking round.

'All right,' Simon grunted. He looked at the GameBoy's small screen and wrinkled his nose. It passed the time, but compared to the game waiting for him back home, it was kids' stuff.

The car headed out of town.

'I expect you'll be gearing up for exams now, Master Simon,' said the chauffeur cheerfully. 'Got a lot of homework?'

Simon settled further down into the cushions and ignored him. The GameBoy was better than nothing. He started to play it half-heartedly.

It was a fifteen-minute drive out of town and up the hill to his home. The rest of the town fell behind and the road headed up the slope, into the trees . . .

The trees!

'Hey!' He sat up suddenly, the GameBoy forgotten. 'Stop! Stop here!'

The driver half looked round. 'Now, Master Simon, you know your father insists I take you straight home . . .'

'Just do it!' Simon shouted. 'Or . . . or I'll come

back here anyway!' They were just below the treeline, near the top of the hill. It wouldn't take long on his bike.

'All right, keep your hair on,' the chauffeur said mildly. The car slowed down and pulled over.

Simon scrambled out almost before the car stopped moving, but for a moment he just stood and looked at the trees. He wasn't sure he wanted to go on. He had robbed the bakery and beaten up the baker – in a game. And at the same time, something freakily similar had happened in real life. Which *had* to be a coincidence.

But supposing it wasn't?

'Want me to come with you, Master Simon?' the chauffeur called, but Simon barely heard him. He started to walk.

It could be coincidence that the same things happened in his game *and* in reality. But surely the real-life thief wouldn't have hidden the stolen money in the same place as Simon's game character? That would be just too much of a coincidence.

So, he would look under the tree where the computer man had buried the money, and he would find it wasn't there, and he would know it was only a game.

But Simon had to admit that part of him was hoping it was, impossibly, true. How cool would that be? To have a game that manipulated reality!

The wood was quiet, nothing but the sound of wind rustling in the leaves. Simon realized that he was breathing heavily. He recognized the sensation. It was what he felt when Mat Frost was gunning for him. It was fear.

Fear that the money wouldn't be there, or fear that it would? He wasn't sure.

His footsteps crunched in the leaves on the ground and he kept his eyes peeled for the tree. The one with the initials carved into the tree bark.

And there it was. The tree. JV and ZD. Simon slowed down, suddenly unwilling to go further. But he made himself do it. He kneeled down by the foot of the tree, and he almost shouted out loud when he saw what was at the base of the trunk.

There was a pine cone nestling on top of some moss between the roots.

Simon felt as if he was looking down on himself from a long way away. He brushed the moss aside, and a damp bank-note rustled against his fingers.

The money had not been wrapped up in anything, and it was grimy from its night in the undergrowth. Simon already knew how much it would be, but he counted it anyway. Mixed twenties and tens and fives and a bunch of coins.

£788.

Simon sat down heavily on the ground, the money between his feet.

'Oh my God,' he said. 'Oh my God.'

Thoughts whirled in his head. The game was real and he was a thief but it was so cool and he controlled a violent criminal but he could be so popular if he could just handle this right and he didn't have to hurt anyone but he had but that had been before he knew and Mat Frost would be so sick and he just had to work it all out and . . .

. . . and, basically, he could do anything.

Simon scooped the money up and climbed back to his feet. Then he walked back to the car, slowly at first, but with more speed as his thoughts and plans crystallized. By the time he got to the car, a new plan was fully formed.

'Back to town,' he said to the chauffeur.

The largest flat screen monitor Simon could get for £788 had a thirty-two inch screen and a silver and black finish. It took up most of his desk, with just enough room for the keyboard, mouse and joypad. He plugged in the last cable and stepped back to admire it. Yes, it looked good. And in a way it was appropriate. It was like saying thank you to the computer, which had helped him get the money in the first place.

A cool breeze blew in through the open window. A faint snatch of music reached his ears, and Simon went over to stand by the curtains. It came from the other side of the trees. From the lake, where Mat and Tom and all their friends were hanging out together. While Simon was here – alone – as usual. Suddenly the new monitor didn't look so great, but he pushed that thought away. He had to stick to the plan that had come to him in the woods. It sounded like they were having a party down there – the kind of party that should be crashed.

'Simon?' said a voice behind him.

He jumped. 'Mum!'

Mrs Down came into the room. She smiled at him and Simon made himself smile back, hoping he looked calm. He wasn't surprised that she didn't notice the new monitor, but he didn't mind. This was the first time in days she had done more than put her head around the door.

'Hello, darling. I wonder if you could give me a hand?'

'Oh, OK!' Simon said. It was only half past six. Mat and the others would be down at the lake for hours, and if helping his mum out now meant that she wouldn't come back to check on him later, it would be worth it. He wanted to be sure he had total privacy for what he had in mind.

The pile of envelopes was slowly growing beside him, and Simon had lost count of the number of paper cuts he had picked up. He looked sourly at his mother across the table as he took another flyer from her. Fold it once, fold it twice, put it in the envelope. And another. Fold it once, fold it twice . . . *This* was why she wanted to spend time with him. Not for his conversation. Not for being her son. Just for his cheap labour.

His mother glanced up and smiled. 'Thank you so much for this, darling. It really helps the charity when we get the mailing done like this.'

'Whatever,' he muttered. Fold it once, fold it twice . . . 'What's it for, anyway?'

'You remember, the Waterfowl Trust?' she said. 'We reintroduced—'

'Yeah, yeah,' he grunted, cutting her off. It had only been a polite question, and yes, he remembered the Trust. The town had once boasted a unique species of waterfowl down by the lake, until it went almost extinct when Simon's parents were children. A couple of years ago, some chicks raised in captivity had been set free in a protected area near the marina, and now the small community was thriving in the wild. Simon's school had raised funds to help it; the fact that Simon's mum had been in charge of the project had given Mat Frost more ammunition then ever in his war against Simon.

'Almost done,' she said. She held up a sheaf of computer printed labels. 'Then we just have to put one of these on each of them—'

Simon shot to his feet. 'Sorry, Mum. Homework to do!' He bolted upstairs two at a time before she could protest.

His room was cold. He had never got round to closing the window. He shot a final look in the direction of the lake, where he could hear the faint thumping of bass music. Then he pulled the window to and turned back to the computer.

'What . . . ?'

The screen was glowing softly. He didn't remember turning the PC on before he went downstairs with his mum. The new monitor's screen was still black but blood-red letters were painting themselves across it with razor-sharp, high res clarity.

Ready to play?

Simon slowly sat down in front of the screen. Too right, he was ready to play. In fact, when he thought about it, he was desperate to play.

He typed, 'Yes'.

The screen cleared to show the man standing in the middle of the park.

We can go to:
- *the cinema*
- *the*

Simon didn't wait for the options. He knew where he wanted to go. He typed, 'LAKE' in capital letters, and pressed return.

OK.

The man on the screen began to run, and Simon picked up the joypad.

He swore when he remembered the major drawback of the game. Everything was in real time, and getting from the park to the lake on the edge of town would take forever. He moved the pad and tried to change the computer's mind, but it seemed set. Simon groaned and sat back in his chair. All he could do was watch the man run.

Daylight was fading – outside, through the window, and on the computer screen. The streetlights came on, but by the time the man reached the lakeside it was almost dark. He walked across the empty car park. The gate in the wire fence that surrounded the marina was locked. The man pressed his face to the wire. The lights in the clubhouse were out and dinghies bobbed silently by the jetties. A light wind was blowing across the water, whipping it into white-topped ripples.

Simon made the man look around. Where was everyone? He wasn't going to hurt them – he just wanted to join in the party, in a way they would never forget.

It was no good. Even though Simon turned the speakers up to maximum, all he could hear was the wind in the trees and the occasional passing car in the distance. The man had taken so long to get here that the party had packed up. Angrily he pounded the computer desk, making the monitor bounce. Why couldn't the stupid man in the stupid game have started at the marina in the first place, before everyone vanished?

They're hiding from you.

Simon wasn't sure if it came from the computer or if the message just popped up in his mind, but he felt the anger swell up inside him. Hiding? From him? How could they! How dare they!

He set the man to run along the shore, looking from left to right, but there was no sign of anyone else about and no sound either. Eventually Simon made him run back to the marina, the only place anyone could be hiding. There were lights in the car park but nothing in the marina; it was dark and shadowed behind its wire fence.

'Come on!' Simon shouted. 'Come and get it!' The man climbed the fence in seconds and dropped down to the other side.

Simon strained his eyes at the screen. It was the same trouble as the end of the game yesterday. It was dark outside, and he could hardly see anything.

'Find them!' he hissed at the man. *'Find them!'*

But the man did nothing, of course, because Simon hadn't moved the joypad.

'I have had it with this stupid game!' Simon yelled at the screen. 'Just as you're getting good, you do this! What's the point?'

As if in answer, white text popped up against the dark background of the screen.

What would you like to do:
- *Sulk*
- *Go to bed with a glass of milk and a kiss from Mummy*
- *Rampage*

'Don't get smart with me,' Simon muttered. Rampage, eh? He selected the last option and clicked. The screen stayed black; he couldn't see the man in the darkness. After a pause, he dimly heard the sound of glass being smashed through the speakers. Then something hard breaking. Then something . . .

But it was still night-time, and he still couldn't see anything. Simon turned the monitor off with an angry jab of his finger.

49

* * *

Simon sat in class, almost in a trance, with the blood roaring in his ears. The teacher was talking, but her voice sounded muffled and a long way off.

He ran again through the sequence of events last night in his mind. He had selected 'Rampage'. But it had been too dark to see anything and he had switched the monitor off. And then it had been morning, and he was getting out of bed (though he didn't remember getting in). And then he had turned on the TV and flicked on the local news channel.

The reporter had been standing on the jetty at the lake. The camera panned across the smashed hulls, the fragments of boat that lay slumped in the water. In a grave voice, the reporter had described how someone had destroyed the dinghies the previous night. Every single boat had been sunk, and the windows of the clubhouse had been smashed in.

But that hadn't been what made Simon scramble for the off-button on the remote. With an apology for the disturbing images, the reporter panned to the nearby waterfowl. An oar from one of the boats lay beside a nest, its blade smeared with feathers and blood. The entire colony had been wiped out, just months after being saved from extinction by Eleanor Down, the reporter explained sombrely. The camera lingered on the tiny, defenceless, broken bodies until Simon pressed the off-button so hard it left a small indentation in his thumb.

And then he had seen that the computer was on. A blank screen with white text.

You did that.

'I didn't!' he said sharply. 'It was him.'

But don't you control him?

Simon jumped almost halfway across the room. 'Of course I control him!'

Then it's still your fault . . .

'It was an accident!' he shouted. 'I didn't know what "Rampage" was going to mean. It won't happen again. From now on I tell him exactly what to do. Exactly!'

'Exactly,' Simon murmured to himself again now, sitting in class.

'I beg your pardon, Simon?' the teacher said.

Simon came back with a start, knocking his pencil-case on to the floor. Pens ricocheted everywhere. The rest of the class, even people that normally left him alone, burst out laughing. But at that moment, it was the least of his worries.

Simon spent most of the day trying to forget about the attack at the marina, and it almost worked.

'Hey, Down!'

Simon groaned. Frost had spotted him when he was halfway out of the door on the way home.

Mat came down the corridor with a malicious grin

on his face. He had the usual crowd of hangers-on with him. 'Sorry you couldn't make it last night, Downy, but we're all right, thanks for asking. We had a great time.'

'That's a shame,' Simon snarled before he could think what he was saying.

Mat's face clouded. 'Hey, Downy boy, what's your problem? I thought you'd be glad we weren't attacked by the mad axeman.'

Simon knew perfectly well that they hadn't been in danger from the mad axeman – they had all gone home before he arrived. The fact that he couldn't tell anyone boiled inside him.

Mat's face cleared as if a great thought had occurred to him. 'Of *course*, they were *Mummy's* birds, weren't they?' he exclaimed. 'Oh, did Mummy cry when she heard the news?'

Simon took a step towards Mat. 'Take that back,' he hissed, 'or . . .'

Mat scowled. 'Or what, nerd?' He casually put a hand on Simon's shoulder and started to walk forward. Simon tried to break free of his grip, but Mat was bigger and stronger and simply shoved him against the wall. Simon glanced helplessly at the circle of Mat's admirers in the background. No one told Mat to cool it. No one did anything to help. Some of them started laughing at Simon as he squirmed, trying to break free. Rage burned inside him. He was in charge of the most dangerous man in town, and they were laughing at him.

Mat leaned forward until their faces were close together. There wasn't the slightest sign of humour in his cold eyes. Simon forced himself to meet his gaze, and imagined the man smashing Mat's face in. To his surprise, he felt himself smile.

Mat's lip curled. 'You really are pathetic, Down,' he growled. Then he let Simon go with a jerk, and walked off. Simon felt the ice grow around his heart as he stalked out to the waiting car.

FROST MOTORS. The sign above the dealership looked exactly as it did in real life. A gleaming row of cars was parked on the forecourt – a couple of Porsches, a Ferrari, a Maserati and a vintage Aston Martin.

The man's axe clanged on to the hood of the Ferrari. He wrenched it out of the dented metal and swung it at the windshield, which shattered into a thousand tiny fragments. The car's alarm whooped repetitively while the man went round to the side and began to swing the axe at the tyres. Each move, Simon was pleased to see, was carried out according to his commands on the joypad. The man was doing as he was told.

Simon was in control.

'Hey!' said a voice through the speaker.

Mechanics and salesmen had started pouring out of the main shop. They fell on the man and dragged him from the car. Simon used the joypad to fight them off. He made sure that the man used the baseball bat that he had brought with him, not the axe. It was a blunt weapon, but not a lethal one. The staff fell back, terrified.

Simon ignored them and steered the man to the next car. He smashed the window and reached in for the handbrake.

Hang on – Simon hadn't given him the command for that! He rattled the joypad angrily. 'No! Wait!'

The man released the brake, put his shoulder to the side of the car and pushed. It rolled forward, slowly at first, then picked up speed as it slid out of the forecourt and on to the main road. Traffic swerved, horns blazing, as it trundled to a stop.

'Now wait a minute!'

The shout came from off screen. The man slowly turned to face Matthew Frost Senior, who was sprinting out from his office. Mr Frost walked up to the man and jabbed him in the chest. On the screen, the man jerked slightly, then stood still.

'The police are on their way,' growled Mr Frost, 'and you are going straight to jail—'

The man reached up and wrapped both hands round Mr Frost's throat.

'No!' Simon gasped. Destroy, yes. Kill? No! He

grabbed the joypad, and snatched his hand away again as a jolt of power almost like a sting went through him. For just a fleeting moment he had been sure he, Simon, was *there*. He was on the forecourt, revelling in what he had done, and what he was about to do.

On screen, Mr Frost let out a horrible gurgling noise, and went limp.

Simon jabbed at the monitor's off-button with a frightened shout. It had no effect; the picture stayed there. He dropped to his knees and scrabbled about under the desk, groping for the power leads. His fingers closed around them, and he yanked them from the socket. The computer went silent. He scrambled back to his feet again, banging his head on the bottom of the desk as he straightened up.

Simon slumped back into his chair again, trembling. He couldn't take his eyes off the monitor, terrified it might switch on again – even though he was still clutching the plug. Had he stopped the game, or was it still going on, in some corner of cyberspace? Was the man still murdering Mat's dad?

But isn't that the point? said that small voice at the back of his mind. *It's the man murdering Mr Frost. You didn't make him do it.*

'No,' Simon murmured. 'I didn't.' He hadn't selected any 'murder' options, hadn't controlled the man's actions. He had just gone there to smash the place up. How was he to blame if the man started acting on his own?

Exploring the thought was a guilty pleasure, like probing a sore tooth with his tongue. Touch it very gently, get a twinge, pull quickly away . . . and then come back for more. Each time it got easier.

Of course, Simon felt sorry for Mr Frost. But honestly, what kind of fool tackles a man like that? Really, he had it coming. Might as well blame a car that killed someone who stepped in front of it. Some things were just inevitable. How else was the encounter going to turn out? Mr Frost should have left the man alone. End of.

And had Simon been at the scene of the crime?

No. Had he left a single fingerprint or DNA sample? Of course not. He could never be accused of anything connected with it.

And he knew something Mat Frost didn't. Where was Mat now? Watching TV, hanging out with his friends? Having a great time, as usual, without caring who he hurt along the way. When he, Simon, knew what had happened to his father.

By now the horror had gone, replaced by a feeling of eerie calm. Simon kneeled down to plug the computer back in, then returned to his chair to wait as the machine whirred back into life.

He wasn't surprised that he didn't need to reload the game. The screen went straight to the forecourt of Frost Motors, and the motionless body that lay there while paramedics tried to revive it. The view was lower down than before, and half obscured by a delivery truck. The man was crouched on the other side of the road from the garage. Simon guessed that he must be hiding from the police.

He quietly switched the machine off again, and turned to his homework.

'Mat Frost's father was killed last night.'

Not a sound broke the silence in the Assembly the next morning. The headmaster delivered his news in solemn tones and a voice that shook ever so slightly. Simon didn't take his eyes from the headmaster's face.

'It appears a vandal attacked his car dealership, and murdered Mr Frost when he tried to defend himself.'

There was a pause as the headmaster took a sip of water and cleared his throat.

'Of course, Mat won't be in today, but Mr Frost was a great friend of this school, so we will have a moment's silence for him.'

Assembly over, the students returned to their classes. The chatter in the corridors was subdued. Old habits made Simon look sideways at anyone who came near him, but there was no need.

Without Mat, there was no one to start the usual persecution.

No Mat! Simon smiled. He could walk down the corridor, and Mat wasn't there to make snide remarks. He could concentrate in class, and Mat wasn't flicking chewed up bits of paper at him. He could put his hand up to answer a question and not hear someone murmur 'nerd'.

Life without Mat had a lot going for it.

The icing on the cake came at breaktime when he heard some boys discussing the murder. Tom Mansbridge was holding forth to the usual band of hangers-on.

'First the guy does in the Porsches, then . . .'

'The Ferrari,' Simon said without thinking. 'He did the Ferrari first.' All eyes turned on him.

'Yeah, and I suppose you were an eyewitness?' Tom snapped.

Simon looked him in the eye. 'He did the hood of the Ferrari in with an axe,' he said in a cold, quiet voice, 'and then he started cutting up the tyres . . .'

'Yeah. That's what I heard,' someone else commented. It was the seal of approval that got everyone's attention. Eager faces turned to Simon, leaving Tom stranded like a rock on the beach as the waves poured away.

'So what else happened?' someone demanded, and Simon simply began to describe the events he had seen. A corner of his mind uncurled and stretched like a cat in the sunshine. If there was a digital counter in his life, he thought, counting the number of friends he had, it had zoomed up from zero to double figures in a matter of seconds.

'How do you know all this?' Tom asked suspiciously, and the lie came as smoothly to Simon's mouth as if it was nothing but true.

'I've got access to this really cool cable channel,' he said. 'You get all the news before the main stations. I could tell you some things about the marina too . . .'

'Hey, yeah, what went on there?'

'Did you get a look at the guy who did it?'

Tom folded his arms. 'Yeah. Tell us about it, Down.'

Simon immediately wished he had kept his mouth shut. He hadn't seen anything at the marina. It had all happened in the dark.

'Well, uh . . .' he began.

Tom smiled, snake-like. 'Yes?'

'Well, uh, the guy . . . he got . . . um . . .' Simon thought furiously. How would the man have smashed the boats up? The birds had been killed with an oar, but what would cause that much damage to the dinghies? Then he remembered the man's weapon of choice at Frost Motors. 'Yeah, an axe,' he said, 'of course! He got an axe, and he went about smashing up the boats—'

'Policeman on the radio said it was an iron pipe,' said Tom. 'They found it in the bushes.' He was staring hard at Simon.

'I, uh . . .' Simon stammered. 'Yeah, I meant a pipe, but hey, that's not important . . .'

'You saw the pipe? On your cable channel?'

'Uh-huh,' Simon lied furiously. 'It was—'

'How long was it?'

'Hey, leave it out,' someone protested to Tom. 'Let him tell us.'

Simon held his hands out about a metre apart. 'About this long, and then—'

'What colour was it?'

Simon rolled his eyes. 'Grey.'

'It was definitely not an axe, then?'

'No it wasn't!' Simon shouted.

'Apparently it *was* an axe,' Tom said with satisfaction. 'It was a big *red* fire *axe* from the clubhouse. That's what they found in the bushes.'

Simon stared at him and felt the crowd's respect draining away.

'B-but . . . the pipe . . .' he said.

'I made the pipe up,' Tom told him. 'Like you did. Come on, guys. Let's leave him in his own little world. Just stay away from ours, will you, Down?'

Tom walked away without looking back, and bit by bit, the crowd around Simon dissolved. Some of them looked back; some with hostility, some just offended.

'That's not funny, Simon,' one of them muttered. Someone else deliberately barged into him, just like Mat used to. Ten seconds later, Simon was on his own again, in the middle of the corridor, his face burning. And the friends counter was back to zero.

His face still burned as the car drove him away from school. He had been telling the truth! How ironic was that? Until smart-alec Tom asked about the marina, he had been describing everything exactly as it happened. The injustice of it made him want to scream. He had been giving them what they wanted, and *still* they rejected him. They didn't want him if he told the truth. They didn't want him if he lied. They just didn't want him.

Let's leave him in his own little world. That's what Tom had said. Well, they could have been part of that world if they had wanted. They could have been his friends. He would have let them into his life if they'd asked. But instead . . .

Just stay away from ours, will you, Down? No way. No way! Simon was going to give their world a message it couldn't ignore.

He walked up to his room, threw his bag on the bed and turned confidently to the computer.

I MISSED YOU, said the letters on the screen. *WELCOME BACK*.

'Let's play!' he said, smiling.

The helicopter plunged to earth with smoke pouring from its engine and the scream of its shattered motor pouring from the speakers. It hit the side of the council offices and exploded in an orange ball of flame.

A muffled *boom* came through Simon's window, mixed with the sound of sirens that had been a continuous background noise for the better part of two days.

The man stood on top of the multi-storey and lowered the rifle. Simon grinned. The traffic helicopter had been hovering over town and annoying him, buzzing around like an oversized insect, sticking its nose in where it wasn't wanted. He – Simon, the man, they were practically the same thing now – had taken matters into his own hands.

Still, Simon supposed he owed the helicopter something. All he could see on screen was what the man could see. The helicopter's last report for the local radio station had been a handy summary of his work so far. 'The weekend that anarchy and destruction came to town,' as the guy in the newsroom had described it.

The town hall was ablaze. Black smoke poured from the windows of one of the department stores. The library was like a furnace with black, charred sheets of paper flying out of the building on the up-draught. Simon's school was a smouldering shell.

Amazingly, it wasn't all the man's doing. The violence was breeding. Simon had been creative. He had started a riot by having the man assault some football supporters on their way home from a match and – just before shooting down the helicopter –

sprung the inmates from the prison's maximum security wing. It all added to the mix.

The townsfolk had taken the hint and all roads out were jammed with fleeing vehicles. It did them little good because the man had blocked the main routes with hijacked lorries.

The computer no longer made suggestions. They had all been Simon's own ideas. It didn't seem to matter what precautions people took down there in the town. If doors were locked, his man could open them. If people came at him, he could fight them off. The man was unstoppable.

Simon was unstoppable.

Oh yes, no one would be forgetting this in a hurry.

Something at the back of Simon's mind told him he was starving and tired and smelly. He hadn't eaten, he hadn't slept, he hadn't washed in two days. All weekend he had been here at the computer, orchestrating the crime wave. And while a small part of his mind screamed in horror at the things he was doing, the rest of it soared in triumph. This felt right.

It felt *necessary*. He knew that what he was doing lurked deep inside everyone's hearts. He was simply setting it free.

The door to his room opened for the first time in two days. Normally the servants just knocked and went away again when there was no answer. Some of the braver ones put their head round the door until he shouted at them. But this time . . .

'Simon?'

'Oh. Hi, Dad.' Simon's father didn't come far into the room. Simon was dimly aware of a tall presence somewhere behind him – which was about all he saw of his father anyway, at the best of times. He didn't budge his eyes from the screen, but he did turn the speakers down. He was running the man up Church Avenue to the museum. Why hadn't he thought of that earlier? The museum was crammed full of important and expensive stuff.

His father wrinkled his nose. 'Can't you open a window? It stinks in here.'

'Whatever,' Simon replied. The man had reached

the glass front doors. The museum was closed and the glass doors were locked against looters. The man picked up a litter bin and threw it at them.

'I'm needed down at the bank. Someone has to pull the security staff together. They're panicking. Don't worry, we'll be safe . . .'

Yeah, yeah, Simon thought, barely listening. *Go away.*

'The car's reinforced, and the driver's been on one of those advanced courses . . .'

'Uh-huh.'

There was the murmur of a woman's voice on the landing outside.

'Oh, and Mum's coming with me,' Dad said. 'But like I say, we'll be safe. We'll be quick, in and out, so don't worry.'

'Fine,' Simon murmured, without taking his eyes off the screen.

Mr Down peered over Simon's shoulder. 'My God, what are you playing?' He swallowed audibly. 'Once all this is over I promise we'll do much more together. Right?'

He put a hand on Simon's shoulder. Simon shrugged it off. His dad sighed. 'I don't like leaving you, but you're better off up here than down in town. See you later, Simon.'

Simon leaned forward to turn the sound back up. On the screen, the man had picked up a small stone statue from the Roman display and was using it as a club to pound the other items to pieces. A security guard ran at him and the man hit him with the stone figure. The guard dropped to the floor and lay still.

Then he moved on to the next gallery in the museum: Medieval Weapons.

You have caused:

* £31,593,476 *of damage.*

Not bad, Simon thought. The man trotted down the steps away from the museum, and Simon sat back in his chair and stretched. He felt his spine click. He twined his fingers together and made them pop. Ah, that felt good.

Hey Simon — where to next?
Why not hit where it's really going to hurt?

Simon frowned. It was the first time in hours that the computer had made a suggestion. What did it mean by 'hitting where it hurts'? Hadn't he already caused over thirty million pounds' worth of damage? That *had* to hurt . . .

A vague memory began to creep into his mind. Hadn't Mum and Dad been in here just now? What had Dad said, something about . . .

Something about going into town.

About going to the bank.

Duh! Simon slapped his forehead. How could he be so slow? To take out the bank — the place that was Dad's reason for living — yeah! It would show Mum and Dad that he was more important than they thought. And if he took all the money in the bank, his score would be humungous!

'Right,' he said, 'we're going to the bank!'

Immediately, the man on the screen broke into

that familiar, long-legged run. Simon was used to it by now. Once he had a destination in mind, the man would just head there. It was boring but—

Simon sat up with a jolt. He hadn't used the joypad to select the destination. He hadn't got any voice recognition gear – how could the computer have reacted to what he said?

He grabbed the pad and tried to bring the man to a halt, but the man just kept running. A gang of thugs looting a TV shop parted to let him through. On past the burning town hall, jump up to run along the roofs of a jammed-up line of cars. On towards the Square, where the bank was.

Suddenly, the man jumped down from the car roofs and ran over to a moving vehicle on the other side of the road. He easily caught it up. He pulled the driver's door open and wrenched the driver from behind the wheel. The driver started to protest, and Simon's man slammed his fists into his stomach, his face. The driver fell to his knees, doubled over. Then the man got into the abandoned vehicle and slammed his foot down on the pedal. Tyres screeched and the car lunged forward.

There was no way to control the man with the joypad now. It was like watching a movie – but one that Simon knew was real . . .

Frightened pedestrians threw themselves out of its way. One of them moved too slowly and the wing of the car clipped her, throwing her up into the air. The picture on the screen shifted to the view through the car's windshield. Simon clutched the edges of his desk as the car swerved.

The car careered down the wrong side of the road, heading for the Square. A large black car, a limo, came into view ahead. It was sticking to the right side of the road, which meant it was barely moving. Something began to tickle at the back of Simon's mind. The limousine looked familiar.

The stolen car swerved towards the limo, picking up speed. Simon shouted a warning. But of course, no one could hear him. The car smashed straight into the side of the limo with a shriek of crushing metal. The windshield of Simon's car disintegrated, and Simon stared out in horror.

A door opened in the limo and a figure staggered out.

'Dad!' Simon shouted at the screen. 'Look out!'

The man reversed the car, then slammed into forward gear again.

Simon screamed. 'NO!'

His father was caught between the front of the stolen car and the side of his limo. A ton of metal smashed into him. The man reversed the car again, and Mr Down's limp, broken body dropped to the ground.

In that split second, Simon was a normal boy again. One look at his dead father cut right through all the hate, all the anger, all the frustration that drove the game, as if they had never been there. Simon felt his stomach heave and had to clutch his mouth. But he couldn't tear his eyes from the screen.

Inside the limo he could see a faint shape, dazed and barely moving, which he knew was his mum.

The car smashed into the limo again, and this time the man kept his foot on the pedal. The limo began to move sideways, shunted across the pavement, faster and faster, until it hit a wall. Then a spark must have caught the petrol tank. There was the *whoomph* of exploding petrol and a ball of fire burst out of the ruined interior. Greedy orange flames licked over the screen.

Simon reeled away from the computer. 'No,' he whispered. 'It's only a game. IT HAS TO BE! It's only a game!' he screamed.

He would check the TV news channel. It *had* to be showing something different. He would know it wasn't real then, and his mum and dad would be back soon.

He flicked the TV on and used the remote to churn through the channels. And there it was. A helicopter view of the Town Square, with his parents' limo lying twisted and burning on one side. His father's body lay on the pavement; a paramedic was just laying a blanket over him. Horrified crowds milled around, abandoning their cars in their panic to get away. There was no sign of the man.

Simon looked at the monitor on his desk. He could see exactly the same scene. Then the man on the screen looked up.

The monitor switched to another view. It showed the man's gaze moving up – past the buildings around the Square, and beyond. Up to the grand house that sat on the hill above the town.

Simon's house.

The man began to run – that long-legged, familiar style – taking the road that led out of town.

'NO!' Simon shouted, leaden fear in the pit of his stomach.

He pelted across the room and slammed into his chair. He ejected the disc tray and snatched up the DVD. He brought it down, hard, against the edge of the table. It didn't break. He put it against the edge of the table and leaned on it with all his weight. The disc began to bend, then suddenly snapped in two. A shard of jagged plastic cut into his wrist.

Simon leaned on the desk, breathing heavily, his eyes closed. He had destroyed the source of the game. It was over. It had to be.

He could still hear sirens through the computer speakers. He opened his eyes, and screamed.

The game was still running.

Simon tried to log off but the computer ignored him. He pressed CTRL-ALT-DELETE and nothing happened. He stabbed at the power switch, but his PC stayed on. He dropped to his knees and scrabbled under the table for the power lead. He yanked it out of the CPU, then for good measure he yanked the other end out of the wall. The game kept running.

The man was near now.

Simon yelled and ran on to the landing. 'He's coming!' he howled down into the hall.

Templeton blinked up at him from the bottom of the long stairway. 'Who is coming, Master Simon?'

'He . . . he is! He killed Mum and Dad. He's coming here—'

The butler frowned. 'Are you all right, Master Simon?'

And then something smashed into the front doors.

'What on earth was that?' Templeton strode over to the doors.

'Be careful!' Simon screamed, retreating. 'He can't be . . . here already.' The man never moved this quick in the game! He ran back into his room. On the battered monitor, he saw the front door open. The butler's staring face filled the screen.

'Who are—'

The man's fist plunged into Templeton's face and he staggered back, blood streaming from his nose. The man followed him into the house and reached out. His fingers locked around the butler's neck and squeezed. Templeton pawed at the man's wrists, trying to break the iron-hard grip. Then his eyes glazed and his body slumped. The man dropped him.

There was a scream from one side. The man

swung round to see the housekeeper standing there, her hands to her face. He moved too quickly for her, lunging and grabbing her before she could get away. He wrapped an arm around her neck and twisted. Her screams stopped abruptly.

Simon sobbed and rushed over to slam his bedroom door. He turned the key and looked around him.

The PC was still, impossibly, on.

The game kept playing.

Simon backed against the wall in terror but he could not tear his eyes away from his PC screen. He could see the man walking up the stairs towards his room. The man reached for the door handle and Simon listened to his ragged breath through the speakers. He looked over at the real door. The handle was turning. It stopped and there was a pause, and suddenly the wooden panels shook as a heavy weight threw itself against them.

And again.

The panels began to splinter.

Tears of terror blurred Simon's vision, and the last thing he saw on the PC screen before the door burst open were the words . . .

Game Over

THE OTHER SISTER

Sparkle Accessories was churning with the usual midsummer crowd. A musical froth of boy band greatest hits played in the background as Catherine Woollams greeted each customer with a bright smile. It felt as fake as the new range of gold and silver lipsticks that she had spent all morning stacking in the window.

A knot of three girls finally made it to the front of the queue.

'Got anything blue?' one of them demanded. They were poking through a pile of hair scrunchies which they had poured out on to the counter top.

'We're out of blue,' Catherine apologized. She pointed out the alternatives. 'We have red, green, yellow, orange . . .'

'Nah . . .' The girl considered. 'Anything sort of turquoisey?'

'No, not really, just what's here – red, green . . .'

'How about navy? Or sapphire! Ooh, I really fancy sapphire . . .'

A corner of Catherine's mind was already running through everything else she had to do. Stock-take the bracelets counter, move the earrings closer to the front door – Stella, the manager, had read in a retail magazine that customers liked to see the cheaper items first as it was less off-putting – reorganize the handbag display . . .

'No,' she said. 'Just red or . . .'

The girl turned away and shoved past her friends.

'Forget it. Come on, you lot. This place sucks.'

Catherine was already giving the next customer a smile, while another corner of her mind took half a second to mutter darkly about timewasters. There was no point in thinking about them for too long, or she would spend all day seething.

Sparkle Accessories had a staff of three, including the manager, and halfway through the summer holidays it was always packed. But Catherine knew how to make each customer feel they were the only one she was concentrating on.

'Can I help you?' she said cheerfully. The woman was at least twice the age of a typical customer, and Catherine wondered if she'd wandered in by mistake.

'At last!' the woman exclaimed. 'I've been standing here for ages.'

'How can I help, madam?' said Catherine.

'I mean, it's not as if everyone has all day to stand around, is it?'

'No, it isn't,' Catherine agreed, her smile

beginning to ache. 'What can I do for you?'

The customer pulled a green scarf from her bag. 'It's this scarf,' she said. 'I bought it a couple of days ago—'

'Got any belts?' asked a girl of about twelve, pushing past the woman.

'Next to the gloves,' Catherine replied automatically, pointing.

'Oh, yeah.' The girl rushed off and Catherine turned back to the other customer.

'Just look at this stitching!' she was saying, holding up the scarf and pointing to the hem. 'It's coming undone already!'

Catherine listened to the woman's complaint with a polite smile. She had been doing this job since she was fourteen, two years ago, when she had started as a Saturday worker. This summer was the first time she had worked here full time, before she started her final year at sixth form college. The last four weeks had given her more practice than she ever thought she'd need in smiling politely, nodding in all the right places, and ignoring everything the customer said.

The woman went on fussily, 'And on top of the stitching problem, when I wore this scarf out in the daylight I realized that it's really a kind of lime green but my colouring is much more jade.'

Catherine nodded and smiled.

'And the way it fits around my shoulders doesn't suit my figure as well as it could . . .'

Doesn't suit your figure? This is Sparkle Accessories! For GIRLS! You're trying to wear a scarf for someone half your age! What do you expect?

'So I thought, if you have something in . . .'

I mean, what were you THINKING?

'Is everything all right, Catherine?'

Catherine's heart sank, though the smile never left her face. Stella, the manager, had wafted out of the stockroom and launched into the conversation. Stella liked to power dress in smart dark suits, with high heels and immaculate hair, making absolutely no secret of the fact that she intended to manage a department store one day.

'Yes, Stella,' Catherine said. 'This lady was just returning a scarf . . .'

'Then I think you should go and choose a selection of alternatives that we can offer madam instead.' Stella beamed at the customer, who nodded. 'Something to suit madam's natural colouring – say, jade?'

The woman smirked, and Catherine thought, *You're only saying that because you heard HER say it.* 'Right away, Stella,' she said, stepping away from the counter.

'And when that's done, I'd like you to move the earrings . . .'

'It's on my to-do list, Stella.'

'Well, *to do* isn't *done*, is it?' Stella replied, as if she was passing on a great wisdom. It was probably a catchphrase she had found in a textbook on retail management. Catherine knew better than to say anything, so she just hurried over to the scarves to pick out anything that was remotely green.

She found three or four and turned back to the counter, nearly cannoning into a small girl who was standing right behind her. The girl hadn't seen her – she was slowly turning a revolving carousel of glittery purses, staring at the way the harsh electric light sparkled on the plastic jewels. Catherine wasn't great at guessing children's ages, but she looked small enough to be about six years old, with untidy shoulder-length dark blonde hair and a bright, padded coat with red and pink patches. It was an unusual pattern, but quite stylish in a bold, retro sort of way. Catherine wondered where the coat came from, and if it came in grown-up sizes.

'Hello,' she said. The girl looked up at her for just a moment, then went back to the carousel. Catherine paused for a moment, thinking hard. Stella didn't like unaccompanied children in the shop – they never had any money to spend, and some of them stole stuff. But this girl looked much younger than most of their problem customers, and Catherine figured that at least one parent must be close by. So she squeezed past, hoisting her fake smile into place again, and went back to the counter.

'Oh, well, I don't know,' the woman said when Catherine fanned the scarves out on the counter. 'These aren't really *jade*, are they?'

Fortunately, Stella seemed determined to make this sale herself, so she was the one who had to persuade the woman that a particular green scarf was the one to match her eyes. Catherine hovered in the background, wondering if she could leave Stella to deal with the rest of the queue and get on with moving the earrings. She looked around the shop to see if the little girl was still there.

She was looking at the display of handbags now, running one finger over a gleaming lilac leather clutch bag. Catherine watched her curiously – the bag was one of the most expensive items in the shop, and she doubted the kid was really intending to buy it. But she didn't want Stella to barge over and order the girl out of the shop, so she kept an eye on her, hoping her parents would appear.

After a couple of minutes, it became clear that the little girl was on her own. Perhaps her parents were in another shop. She didn't look like she was going to be a problem. Catherine had had trouble before with kids who had grabbed something that took their fancy and rushed out through the detectors by the door, setting the alarm off but too late to be caught. But this little girl seemed too young, too shy and quiet, to do a grab and run.

Finally the difficult customer departed with a scarf that was as close a match to her eyes as Sparkle Accessories could offer. Stella vanished into the stockroom since Beth, the other full-time shop assistant, had returned from her lunch break to battle with the rest of the queue.

'Be with you in a moment, Beth,' Catherine promised, heading over to the little girl. She had reached a display of rainbow-coloured gloves and was looking at them wistfully, as if she didn't dare actually reach out and touch them.

Catherine put on her best smile – one that almost felt genuine – and squatted down beside her. 'Hi,' she said. 'Are you looking for anything in particular?'

The girl looked up at her. Her expression was closed and shy but there seemed to be a smile there, hovering behind her wide, brown eyes. Her fingers brushed against one of the gloves. 'I like these,' she murmured, so quietly that Catherine had to strain to listen.

'I think they might be a bit expensive for you, I'm afraid,' Catherine told her gently.

The girl looked crestfallen. 'I don't have any money. But . . .' she leaned closer, '. . . my sister would really like them.' She said it as if she was sharing the world's greatest secret. Catherine drew a breath to ask about the sister – was she older or younger? Was she with her mummy and daddy? In fact, *where* were her mummy and daddy? But then she heard Stella calling briskly across the shop.

'Catherine! What are you doing over there? Come and help Beth! Efficient staff are busy staff!'

Catherine straightened up. 'I'm just coming, Stella.'

Stella opened her mouth to say something else, and Catherine saw her lips purse as she spotted the little girl.

'I hope . . .' she began, and Catherine knew she was about half a second away from being reminded about the policy for unaccompanied children.

'I'm sorry, these are for the paying customers,' she muttered, pushing the gloves away from the girl's hands. 'I think you should go and find your parents.' Out of the corner of her eye she saw Stella nod approvingly and turn away.

The girl held her gaze for a moment with dark, expressionless eyes, before brushing past her and running out of the shop. The gloves swung slightly on the display stand, and Catherine felt about an inch tall.

Well, what was I supposed to do? she thought angrily – angry with herself, angry with Stella, even angry with the girl. *She couldn't just hang around, she obviously wasn't going to buy anything and if she had tried to run off with something, Stella would have blamed me entirely!* She sighed, wondering if it was too late to find a job that didn't involve dealing with the general public, or over-ambitious managers, and went back to the counter.

Two days later, Catherine pushed her way hurriedly through the automatic doors into the shopping mall. It was busier than usual for a Monday, packed with people who seemed determined to walk ten times slower than she wanted to. She had overslept, the bus had crawled through heavy traffic into the town centre, and she had about three minutes left before she was officially late for work.

'Excuse me . . . sorry . . . thanks . . .' she murmured breathlessly, pushing and dodging her way to the escalator leading up to the first floor.

'Excuse me . . .' She tried to squeeze past the person in front of her on the escalator, hoping she could run up, and the man scowled over his shoulder at her.

'What's the big hurry? You do know these stairs move, don't you?' he snapped, and then looked away, stubbornly refusing to let her get past. Catherine gritted her teeth as she was forced to ride the rest of the way up at the same leisurely pace as everyone else.

Suddenly, a flash of pink and red caught her eye. Something in the pattern reminded her of the child she had seen on Saturday. Catherine gazed around, standing on tiptoe to look over the handrail, and then she saw her. The girl was below her, on the ground level, standing by the base of the ornamental fountain.

Catherine thought back to how they had parted – she had almost chased the girl out of the shop, just to avoid Stella's wrath. She wondered if she should go down and apologize, since she hadn't liked having to act that way. She didn't want the little girl to think Sparkle Accessories was staffed by ogres.

'Hello!' Catherine called, as the escalator carried her behind a pillar. She tried to move back a step on the escalator, but it was too crowded and she got a hostile stare from the woman behind her. She couldn't move forward either. And by the time the escalator had moved past the pillar, the girl was gone.

Catherine hurried off the escalator and leaned down over the rail, trying to spot the girl on the level below. The pink coat was nowhere to be seen. She shrugged. It had been a good intention, but not worth worrying about now. And if she didn't get to the shop in the next thirty seconds, she really would be late.

Tuesday felt like a long day, Wednesday even longer. The school holidays meant that a lot of kids had time on their hands, and Catherine could swear that every one of them came into Sparkle Accessories to run ice-cream-sticky fingers over the scarves and muddle up the bracelet display. By the end of the day, every part of her seemed to ache: her feet from standing behind the counter; her throat from speaking over the hubbub of teenage girls and loud music; her head from always having to talk to at least three customers simultaneously, as well as making sure that everything that left the store was paid for, and keeping Stella generally happy. At closing time she was glad to go on to autopilot, to head out into the home-going crowd and shuffle along with everyone else to the exits.

The shopping centre exit led out into the main street. Wednesday was late-night shopping, so it was dark outside by the time Catherine left. The plate glass of the sliding doors looked black and shiny, perfectly reflecting the bright interior of the shopping centre back at her. It was like there were two Catherines walking briskly towards each other, and she took a critical look at her reflection. Her shoulder-length hair could do with being straighter, and she didn't like the way it kinked out more on one side than the other. She bared her teeth to check she hadn't got any lipstick on them, then smiled for real when she realized she looked like a grinning chimp.

The smile vanished when she saw the flash of pink and red again; in the reflection, it was almost right behind her. The girl was standing only a few metres away, and their reflected gazes met for a moment.

Catherine stopped abruptly and turned round, and the woman behind bumped straight into her.

'Sorry!' Catherine gasped, but she was already ducking her head, trying to see past the woman to find the girl. 'I just . . . um . . .'

'It's all right,' the woman said in a tone that said it very clearly wasn't, and she stepped around Catherine and carried on.

Catherine tried for a moment to head back against the crowd, but she had no idea which direction to go. The girl had been swallowed up in the wave of people leaving the shopping centre, and even though Catherine stood on tiptoe and craned her neck, she couldn't spot the small blonde head or the pink and red coat.

'Get a grip, Cath,' she muttered to herself. It really wasn't that important if Sparkle Accessories had lost one small window-shopper. She turned back to the doors and let them slide open in front of her, to release her from another day.

'OK, everybody! It's Friday! Here's something to get you in the dancing mood . . .'

The local radio station was playing merrily in the shop when Catherine walked in, and for once it matched her buoyant mood. Friday at last! OK, so it was the day before Saturday, which was the busiest of the week, but she was still looking forward to the weekend. The atmosphere was always better in the shop, and she had a party at her friend Jenny's house to look forward to on Saturday night. And Jenny had a particularly nice older brother called Chad who was almost certainly going to be there . . .

Catherine's first customer of the day was a rather lost-looking woman about the same age as Catherine's mum. 'School's starting in a couple of weeks . . .' she began.

Don't I know it, Catherine thought gloomily. 'Worst luck!' she said brightly, and the woman smiled.

'. . . and I'd like to get something sort of back-to-school for my daughter's birthday, she's nearly fourteen, but I have absolutely no idea what to get her . . .'

'What does she normally take to school?' Catherine asked.

'Well, her bag, of course, but it's getting a bit tatty.'

'Let's start there, then!' Catherine said, leading the woman over to the bag section.

With the rest of the shop virtually empty, it was a pretty good way to start the day. Catherine enjoyed helping the woman choose not just a new bag but a sparkly pencil-case, a lilac hair scrunchie and a notebook with a glittery, striped cover.

'Oh, and some of those pens!' the woman said.

'Good idea!' For once, Catherine remembered why her job wasn't that bad. The woman paid with her credit card, thanked Catherine over and over, and left with her laden carrier bags. *Why couldn't Stella ever be around to see the grateful customers?* Catherine wondered.

Suddenly, she got the distinct feeling that she was being watched. She spun around to find the little girl in the pink and red coat standing right behind her.

'Oh, hi!' Catherine said. 'Long time, no see!' It was meant as a joke. The girl just looked solemnly up at her.

'So . . .' Catherine thought quickly about what she could say. She didn't want the girl to think she was going to hustle her out again. 'I'm Catherine.'

The girl stared pointedly at Catherine's name tag. 'I'm nine. I can read.'

Nine? Catherine was a bit surprised. She had guessed about three years younger than that. The child was certainly small for her age. But nine was still a bit young to be out shopping on her own.

She looked around – inside the shop, and through the windows into the mall – trying to find an adult who looked like they might belong to the little girl. There didn't seem to be anyone. 'Are you all on your own?' she asked brightly. 'No mummy or daddy?'

The girl picked up a glittery, cat-shaped purse and ran her finger along its spiky plastic whiskers. 'It's OK, you don't need to worry about them,' she shrugged.

'Oh, right,' said Catherine, not sure what else to say.

The girl stared around the shop. 'Everything here's so beautiful,' she said. 'I wish me and my sister could have beautiful things like this. But Mummy won't let us.'

'Um . . . is your sister around?' Catherine asked.

'Hey, Cath!'

Catherine jumped, afraid that she was about to get told off for wasting work time. But it wasn't Stella

– it was Jenny and Helen, from her college.

'There she is!' Helen had spotted Catherine from the doorway, and they homed in on her like missiles in denim.

'Oh, Cath, we so totally need your help, we absolutely have to get something for my party!' Jenny began.

Catherine glanced down at the girl and flinched. The child's wistful expression had gone, replaced by what looked like anger.

'What do they want?' she said.

'Hey, they're my friends!' Catherine protested.

The girl looked up at her with eyes that were cold and hard. 'In that case, I suppose you'd better talk to them,' she said, her voice thin and icy. Shoving the cat-shaped purse back on to the stand, she walked out of the shop before Catherine could say another word, pushing past the two girls coming the other way.

'Who was that weird little kid?' Helen asked, watching the girl's retreating back.

'She's not weird, Hel,' said Catherine, a bit surprised to find herself jumping to the girl's defence. After all, the reaction to Jenny and Helen had definitely been a bit offbeat. 'I think she's just lonely. She's often hanging around, and I've never seen her parents . . .'

'Hey, you two, stop gassing, this is an emergency!' Jenny told them. But Catherine had seen a customer hovering by the counter.

'Look, guys, I have to go and serve that girl. Why not look around and see if there's anything you like?' she suggested. Leaving Jenny and Helen examining the stack of gold and silver lipstick, she hurried over to the till.

'I want to return this hair-band,' the customer explained. She took out a hair-band, glittery and lilac-coloured, and put it on the counter. 'I think some of the sequins are loose.'

Catherine checked; it was hard to tell, but one or two of the sequins were sewn on less tightly than the others. 'Sorry about that,' she said. 'If you like, I could swap it for another?'

'Thanks, if you could,' the girl replied. To Catherine's relief, she didn't sound too annoyed. It was a mystery to her, the things customers got hung up about.

It was a straight swap, old for new, and the girl went away looking perfectly satisfied. Across the store, Jenny and Helen were trying on hats and squealing at how they looked in the mirror. Catherine knew it could take forever before they decided on something. In the meantime she twisted the faulty hair-band in her hands and looked at it thoughtfully.

'*When I'm not with you-u-u . . .*' Catherine sang along to the radio on Monday morning. She stood on tiptoe on a small set of steps, arranging alternating bottles of perfume and nail gloss on a shelf in the window. '. . . *then I'm nowher-r-r-re, because you-u-u are the only-y-y-y . . .*' The song had been echoing in her head all weekend, and not just because it was the current number one. It had been playing when Jenny's brother, Chad, had looked at her from across the room at the party – OK, so he'd gone out to meet his friends before she had a chance to talk to him, but their eyes had definitely met in a meaningful way and she hadn't stopped thinking about him since.

'Are your *friends* here?'

Catherine jumped. The girl stood at the foot of the steps, her neck craning up to look at Catherine. Her eyes were cold and hard, and the way she said *friends* made it sound like an insult.

'No. No, they're not.' Catherine climbed down from the steps. *This is starting to fall under the heading 'weird'*, she thought, remembering what Helen had said on Friday. The girl sounded as if she was bitterly jealous of Helen and Jenny.

'That bottle isn't straight,' said the girl, pointing. Catherine looked up and saw that one of the nail gloss bottles was slightly out of line.

'Thanks,' she said, climbing back up the steps and

reaching out to nudge the bottle with the tip of her finger.

'They were here for ages,' the girl went on. 'I watched through the window. I saw the lady with the hair-band, too.'

'Well, good for you,' said Catherine. She had had an idea about what to do with the hair-band on Friday. But now, with the girl being so hostile, she wasn't sure. On the other hand, this girl might have really strange parents – they were obviously happy to let her wander around town on her own for days on end. It wouldn't take too much effort for Catherine to be friendly. 'Look,' she said. She climbed down again and reached behind the counter. She held out the lilac hair-band. 'I kept it for you.' She knew it would only be thrown away otherwise.

At once the girl's expression was transformed. The ice melted from her eyes, and they became deep and soft and warm. A warm, glowing smile spread across her face.

'Oh!' she breathed. She reached out slowly for the band, as if she was afraid it would break, and slowly lifted it from Catherine's fingers. 'Oh,' she said again. 'It's so *beautiful*! Is it really for *me*?'

'Well, sure . . . um, yes. For you.' Catherine felt quite embarrassed, not just because the girl was so grateful but because, really, the gift wasn't all that special. A reject hair-band wasn't exactly the crown jewels, though the girl was reacting as if it was.

'It's so lovely!' said the girl. 'It's the best present I've *ever* had!' She gazed up at Catherine with an adoring stare that made her blush. 'Thank you so, so much!' Then her face fell. 'I haven't got anything to give you, though.'

'That's OK,' Catherine said quickly. 'You don't have to give me anything.' Her heart twisted. Hadn't anyone ever given this child a present just for the fun of it? Did she always assume there'd be a catch – that she would have to give something in return?

Catherine leaned forward as if she was sharing a secret. The girl smiled more widely and drew closer. Catherine lowered her voice. 'Look, my manager's going to be back soon and she doesn't like kids hanging around without buying anything. But you're welcome to pop in when she's not around.'

The girl smiled again. 'OK.' She pushed the band into her hair and straightened up proudly with her hair tucked neatly behind her ears. 'And I'll wear this all the time!'

She walked away with her head held high.

Catherine remembered something. 'I still don't know your name!' she called.

The girl looked back from the door. For a moment she looked wary, as if she was thinking about what to say.

'Susan,' she said at last, and disappeared into the mall.

'OK . . . OK . . .' Stella was running around like a demented bee, which was her usual state of mind before a visit to the bank. 'Letter? *Letter?* Oh God, where did I put that letter . . . ?'

'By the till,' Catherine told her, not looking up from the box of spiky hair clips that she was sorting. The clips were fiddly and kept jabbing her fingers.

'Oh, yes. I'm going to be late, where's my bag? Where's my *bag?* Oh, thank you, Beth . . . Right, I should be back by two, see you . . .' Stella said breathlessly, and she rushed out, her heels rapping on the floor.

Beth and Catherine looked at each other, and when the sound of clicking heels faded, breathed out sighs of relief.

'Thank goodness for that!' Beth exclaimed. 'I'll make some coffee.' She disappeared into the back room and Catherine carried on with the clips.

'Beth,' she called, 'would you mind being here on your own at lunch?'

'On my own?' Beth reappeared in the doorway. 'Got a secret date, Cath?' Then she saw Catherine going red and her eyes widened. 'No way! You have! Who is it? Tell me everything!'

'It's . . .' Catherine shrugged, but she didn't want to say 'it's nothing', because it was something. 'My friend Jenny called last night and she wants us to meet for lunch . . .' She tried to sound casual, but she could hear the rising excitement in her own voice. '. . . and her brother's going to be there and Jen is sure he's going to ask me out!'

'Oh, Cath!' Beth hugged her. 'That's fantastic! Sure, I can cover for you. But you have to tell me every single detail when you come back! Promise?'

'I promise,' grinned Catherine, feeling her stomach flip over with nerves.

Thirty minutes later, she pulled on her coat and grabbed her bag, stopping by the door to check her lip-gloss for the twentieth time.

'Good luck!' Beth called, giving her a thumbs-up. Catherine smiled back, too excited to speak. She was about to open the door when she saw Susan looking at her through the glass. The band was on her head, a sparkly violet stripe against her blonde hair.

But then Susan saw the coat and the bag and her smile faded, changing into a mask of disappointment.

Catherine pulled the door open, and Susan looked up at her. Her face was a blank mask by now. 'I really need to talk to you,' Susan announced.

'Well, actually . . .' Catherine began, tightening her grip on her bag. She was about to explain that she had a lunch date.

Susan shrugged and turned away. Underneath the hair-band, her hair looked dirtier than ever, and there was a greasy stain on the shoulder of her coat. 'Whatever,' she said.

She sounded so emotionless, so far from caring, that Catherine guessed she was used to disappointment. *Too* used to it. Jenny – and Chad – would be around for other lunches, she told herself. 'But I can cancel,' she went on firmly, and instantly the beam was switched back on in Susan's eyes.

Catherine pulled out her mobile. 'Just give me a minute . . .'

'So what would you like?' Catherine asked, looking down at her companion. They were in the sandwich bar on the ground level. She deliberately hadn't gone to the coffee shop on the top floor in case they bumped into Jenny and Chad. Catherine had told them Stella was making her work through her lunch-hour. There was no way she could let them know she was standing them up for a nine-year-old girl. Right now, every part of Catherine wanted to be on the top floor, having lunch with Jenny and her brother. But Susan had looked so miserable, and she had said she wanted to talk to Catherine, so there must be something important going on.

The little girl seemed to have recovered. 'Chocolate milk-shake,' she said with satisfaction.

'Two chocolate shakes,' Catherine said to the woman behind the counter.

'Here you are,' said the woman a minute later,

handing over two glasses and a cookie for Susan. She passed Catherine her change and smiled at Susan. 'Oh, what a lovely hair-band! Did your sister give it to you?'

Catherine looked down at Susan. Their eyes met and they both dissolved into giggles. They headed for a table without correcting the woman's mistake.

'I always wanted a sister like you,' said Susan when they were sitting down.

'Oh, thanks. Hang on – don't you have a sister?' Catherine said, puzzled.

The girl shrugged and started crumbling her cookie between her fingers.

'Look, Susan,' Catherine tried again. 'Who looks after you? Where's your mum? Or your dad?'

The girl smiled faintly, and didn't look up from her cookie. There were more crumbs than biscuit now, and she started picking out the chocolate chips, lining them up around the edge of the plate. 'I can look after myself, you know,' she said.

'I know, but . . .' Catherine said.

Susan's straw gurgled as she finished her milk-shake, and she slid off her stool. 'That was lovely,' she said. 'Can we do it again tomorrow?'

Catherine sighed. If there was something difficult occurring in the girl's home life – maybe even something perfectly normal, like her mum and dad going through a divorce – then she obviously wasn't ready to talk about it. Maybe she just needed a friend to hang out with, to make her feel wanted. But in the meantime, she had blown a date with Chad for *this*.

'Sure,' Catherine said, forcing herself to smile. 'Come by the shop at the same time. Stella's usually gone out by then.'

'OK, I'll be there!' Susan flashed Catherine a shy smile before pulling on her pink and red coat and vanishing into the crowd.

'Hey! Hello! Over here!' Catherine snapped out of her daydream. The customer was Toni Parker, a girl from Catherine's class that Catherine had never got on with. She waved her hands in front of Catherine's face to get her attention.

'Sorry, I was—'

'Never mind what you were doing, this is important,' Toni snapped. Catherine bristled and felt her fake smile slipping like lipstick under a hot light. 'Look, this handbag is just so unsuitable. It's too small for my purse, it's too small for my mobile, it's—'

'It's a party handbag,' Catherine pointed out. 'It's only meant to be decorative.'

'But where do I put my *mobile*?' Toni complained. 'Look, I want something bigger but *no way* am I paying any more.'

It was almost the end of Catherine's lunch-hour, and there was still no sign of Susan. Perhaps something, or someone, was preventing her from turning up. Perhaps one of her parents had finally discovered a sense of responsibility. Or perhaps, with a kid's typically small attention span, she had simply forgotten. Catherine tried not to feel hurt. She'd thought she'd formed some sort of bond with the lonely little girl, but maybe it had been a one-way thing. *Where was she?*

'You're not listening to me, are you?' said Toni. 'You are so useless, Cath!'

At that moment, as if summoned by poor customer service, Stella came in. 'Ah, Catherine. Is everything all right?'

'Are you the manager?' Toni demanded. 'Maybe you can help.' She pushed the offending handbag along the counter towards Stella.

Catherine had had enough. She was starving, and it had just occurred to her that maybe Susan had got confused. She might have thought they would meet at the sandwich bar, like before, not in the shop. She might be waiting there now, wondering where Catherine was, thinking she'd been forgotten about . . .

'I'm just popping out, Stella,' Catherine said, reaching under the counter for her bag.

Stella stared at her in amazement. 'Catherine, your lunch-hour is twelve-thirty to one-thirty, and it is now . . .' she checked her watch, ' . . . one thirty-seven. So you are not going anywhere.'

'But Beth said she'd cover for me!' Catherine hadn't had the nerve to tell Beth what had really happened the day before, so she had said Chad had cancelled at the last minute – but wanted to see her today instead. Beth had been quite happy to stand in.

Stella folded her hands and Toni grinned smugly behind her.

'Beth can stand in for you during your *approved* lunch break,' Stella lectured, 'but not while you just slope off.'

Slope off! Catherine wanted to shout. *I work like a slave here and I never complain, and now you say I'm sloping off?*

'Look, it's just for a couple of minutes!' she insisted. 'I've worked all through lunch break, so I'm owed a bit . . .'

'Well, you should have *taken* your lunch break. I'm not a slave-driver, Catherine, I just have certain expectations. Now, put your coat down and get back to work. It's bound to get busy once everyone's finished *their* lunch.'

Catherine wavered, and almost gave in. But the thought of Susan waiting hopefully for her was just too much. She would probably stay at the sandwich bar until closing time, convinced that Catherine would turn up at any minute. She'd obviously been let down so many times in her life already; there was no way Catherine was adding to the list of disappointments.

'Just a couple of minutes,' she said, and headed for the door.

'*Catherine!*' Stella's voice was sharp behind her. 'If you leave now I will have no choice but to fire you.'

Catherine hesitated, but the image of Susan, alone and disappointed, filled her mind. She grabbed her jacket and walked out of the shop. Stella wouldn't really fire her. It was the middle of the school holidays, the shop's busiest time. Where else would she get someone willing to put up with her at short notice?

When Catherine reached the sandwich bar, there was no sign of Susan. Catherine swore under her breath and went back to the shop. And found Stella really had fired her.

Hi, Cath!!! Spain is so cool!!!! Boyz <u>everywhere</u>!!!! Hel's dad wants us to see a museum ☹☹☹ but tonight is CLUB NIGHT!!!!!!!!!!!! Love Jen & Hel

'Are they having a nice time in Spain?' Catherine's mum asked as she cleared away the breakfast things. It was a week since Catherine had been fired. Normally, she would have been in the shop for nearly an hour by now, and would be thinking about the first coffee and Danish run of the morning.

'Hard to say,' Catherine muttered. She dropped the postcard on the table and sipped her tea. Jenny and Helen had invited her on the trip back at the start of the holidays, when Helen's parents booked the villa. But Catherine had turned it down because she'd just landed the job at Sparkle Accessories and had *thought* she would be working.

'Well, it's no use moping, dear,' said her mum. 'Maybe you should find some other friends to hang around with.'

'I do have other friends,' Catherine snapped, though off the top of her head she couldn't think of any that she particularly wanted to see. Maybe she had been working too hard at Sparkle Accessories. The only other person she had seen much of recently was . . .

'I met this girl called Susan,' she said, carefully not mentioning the girl's age.

'Well, that's nice! Why don't you invite her over?'

'Um . . .' This hadn't occurred to Catherine before, mainly because she tended not to hang out with nine-year-olds at home. And anyway, she still didn't know where Susan lived. 'I can't, I don't have her number.'

'Not that great a friend, then,' her mum replied, briskly wiping the table with a damp cloth.

Catherine fiddled with her piece of toast and kept quiet. She didn't want to get into a big conversation about her new friend. She'd never been able to lie convincingly to her parents, and she'd only end up giving her mum the impression she'd been hanging around in a kindergarten during her lunch-hour.

In short, it was best not to think of Susan at all. Or Stella. Or being broke. Soon Catherine, Jenny and Helen would be back at college, and she probably wouldn't even remember this depressing school holiday.

'You need to get out more,' her mum said decisively. 'Look, you haven't got your books for sixth form yet, have you? Why not hit the bookshop before everyone else gets there? Don't worry, I'll lend you the money.'

Catherine dropped her uneaten toast back on to the plate and pushed back her chair. Why not? It wasn't like she had anything better to do. 'Thanks, Mum.'

* * *

It seemed odd to find the shopping centre hadn't changed a bit. Catherine had to remind herself it had only been a week. She joined the crowd on the escalator – for once, more than happy to stand still and let the stairs do the work – and admitted that this had been a good idea of her mum's. The busy, upbeat atmosphere was already making her feel better, and it was nice to be here as a customer, not a worker.

She glanced at Sparkle Accessories as the escalator carried her up to the second floor. Maybe she wouldn't go back just yet. Fortunately the bookshop was on the level above, and she was pretty confident she wouldn't bump into Stella in there. The only books she read were delivered by FedEx and had titles like *How to Succeed in Retail Management,* and *Shop Management to the Top: A Store-Fire Way to Win!*

Catherine stopped and browsed the display in the bookshop window. There was a three-for-two offer on her favourite series. She was just calculating if the money her mum had lent her would stretch this far when something made her look up. There it was again — a flash of red and pink in the crowd in the glass. For just a moment Catherine saw Susan, standing not far off and watching her silently. She stiffened, then closed her eyes and groaned.

'Go away,' she murmured. 'Just go away. You've got me into enough trouble.' When she opened her eyes, Susan wasn't there any more. She smiled, trying not to feel like she'd been overreacting. It probably hadn't been Susan at all. That couldn't be the only pink and red coat in the world. She just had Susan on the mind.

'Catherine!'

Someone grabbed her hand and Catherine just managed not to shriek. As if last week hadn't happened, Susan was clinging to the end of her arm, trying to pull her away.

'Catherine, you've got to come!' she gasped before Catherine could say anything. Her voice was high and urgent and her eyes were red, as if she had been crying. She tugged again, practically hopping with impatience. 'Now!'

'Susan, I . . .' Catherine trailed off helplessly. 'Where have you been?'

'Please!' Susan begged. 'You have to come! You have to come and help Laura.'

'Laura?' Catherine echoed. 'Who's Laura?' Something in Susan's tone told her this wasn't a childish game. And now she looked more closely, Susan looked even less cared-for than before. The lilac hair-band was still firmly in place, but her blonde hair hung in lank, greasy rats' tails. And – Catherine's eyes narrowed when she saw it – there was a crusted stain of something red on the front of her coat. Was it *blood*?

'She's my sister! *Please!* She . . . I can't . . . I've got to . . .' Distress was making her stumble over her words and she broke off, putting her hands up to her face.

Catherine made up her mind. Susan clearly needed her help, and whatever it was, it was urgent.

Her mind flooded with images of domestic accidents, the sort that happened to unsupervised children – saucepans of boiling water, heavy items of furniture toppling over . . . 'OK,' she said, turning away from the shop and taking Laura's small sticky hand. 'Lead the way.' They hurried towards the escalator. 'Where is Laura?'

'She's in real trouble,' Susan sobbed.

'Yes, but *where* . . .'

'*Real* trouble.'

Catherine gave up. Susan was too upset to talk sensibly. She just needed to give her time, show that she was on her side, and she would find everything out.

Catherine did her coat up as they half walked, half ran across the car park. She began to warm up, even though it was a cool day for August, and unbuttoned it again. She still didn't know where Susan lived; she had no idea how long this journey was going to take, or even if they were going to run all the way.

126

'I really missed you,' Susan said. Her voice trembled. 'Where did you go?'

'Where did I . . .?' Catherine was so astonished that she slowed down for a moment. She sped up again when Susan tugged at her hand. 'I had to stop working at the shop,' she said eventually. Susan wouldn't understand about being fired, and Catherine didn't intend to make her feel like she was in any way to blame.

They ran through the centre of the town, dodging the too-slow pedestrians and darting across roads, perilously close to moving traffic. Catherine realized they were heading towards the far side of town from where she lived. They'd gone at least a mile but Susan hardly seemed to notice. She didn't even seem to be breathing hard. *She must be really worried about Laura*, Catherine thought. After ten minutes they reached the common and hurried down a footpath that tunnelled under the railway embankment.

'Where are your parents?' Catherine panted as they emerged on the other side. 'Do they know that

Laura's in trouble?' They were in a road she didn't know, with rows of semi-detached houses on either side.

'They're never at home – well, not any more,' Susan said. Somehow this didn't surprise Catherine at all.

'Look,' she insisted, 'you still haven't told me what's wrong with your sister . . .'

Susan's eyes filled with tears again. 'She's in real trouble!' she wailed.

'Yes,' Catherine said, starting to feel frustrated, 'but . . . and, look, I still don't know about your mum or dad . . .'

Susan stopped dead. 'We're here,' she said, her voice very calm.

They were on the corner of two roads. A gravel drive led up to a tall, three-storey house of slightly decaying red brick, set back from the street. The large garden was surrounded with bushes and trees, and the roof was steeply pitched, with ornate gables at either end.

'Wow,' Catherine breathed, forgetting for a moment why they had come. 'You live here?'

Susan was already running up the drive, her feet crunching on the gravel. She glanced back. 'Come *on!*' Her voice quavered, like she was on the verge of tears. Yet she had seemed perfectly composed a moment ago. Catherine frowned to herself. Susan really did have the most up-and-down emotions she had ever known, even for a child. She hurried after the little girl.

A flight of shallow stone steps led up to a front door decorated with stained glass.

'We have to go round the back,' said Susan, and she disappeared along a narrow path around the corner. Catherine looked up at the house slightly nervously as she followed the sound of the girl's rapid footsteps. All the windows were blank and grimy, giving away no clues as to what might be inside. The garden looked so overgrown and neglected that it was hard to believe anyone lived here at all, certainly not Susan's parents.

Catherine felt her heart begin to thud. Was this really where Susan lived? She couldn't get rid of the feeling that she was about to be thrown out for trespassing.

The kitchen door at the back of the house was plain wood, painted green. It was already ajar and Susan slipped inside without looking back.

Catherine hesitated on the threshold. She couldn't just walk into someone else's house. 'H-hello?' she called. 'My name's Catherine. I'm with Susan . . .' She put her hand on the door and it swung open. She took a breath – *This is it! I am now officially an intruder!* – then took another deep breath and walked inside. 'Hello?' she called again. Then she stopped dead.

'Oh . . . my . . .'

The kitchen was filthy. Dirty crockery was piled in the sink, crusty with old food and half submerged in grey scummy water. The tiled floor was covered with muddy footprints and there was an indefinable smell of rot in the air, as if someone had left the lid off a dustbin. A small pile of ragged jam sandwiches sat on a plate on the table with a large kitchen knife next to them. One of the sandwiches had a set of small bite marks in it.

'Is the whole house like this?' Catherine asked in horror. She knew that this was a case for the social services. She had assumed Susan's parents were too busy to look after her. But *this* bad? This much neglect? No, she hadn't expected this.

'Laura's this way,' Susan said. She stood in the far doorway and beckoned. Catherine bit her lip. This was starting to feel way over her head. Supposing one of the parents came home? Could she handle them? Would they get violent? She could imagine the headlines on the news: 'Police are looking for sixteen-year-old Catherine Woollams who has not been seen since yesterday ...'

Susan's bottom lip began to quiver. 'Please, Catherine, hurry!'

Feeling a bit unreal, as if she was in a movie, Catherine walked forward. She passed a pile of washing lying in a basket. It was damp and smelled of mildew.

Susan led her down a short passageway into the hall. Daylight shone through large windows either side of the front door. It had clearly once been very grand; now it was just shabby. Not as bad as the kitchen, but when Catherine ran her finger along the top of the hall table, she left a clear track through the layer of dust. The hallway was lined with wooden panels that made her footsteps echo on the tiled floor, loud as heartbeats. Catherine felt the house looming around her, the windows' eyes watching her every move, the staircase a gaping throat ready to swallow her up.

Susan stopped by a door set into the wall under the stairs. She rested her hand against the wood.

'Laura's in here,' she whispered, her eyes huge. 'They locked her in.'

'Under the stairs?' Catherine couldn't believe it. Or maybe, having seen the kitchen, she could.

'This door goes down to the cellar,' Susan

explained earnestly, as if that somehow wasn't as bad as being locked in a cupboard. A fat tear rolled down her cheek. 'Mummy says Laura is evil and can't be allowed out, otherwise she'll hurt people.'

'*Evil!?*' Catherine choked. She felt hot and cold all at once, and suddenly the feeling of unreality vanished and she knew she was truly here, right now. Surrounded by some nameless horror that made her breath feel tight and her skin clammy . . .

'Laura's my twin. Mummy and Daddy hate her because she didn't clean the bathroom properly.' Susan began to cry, her small frame shaking with sobs. 'But she's not evil, and . . . and . . . I was meant to clean the kitchen, and I haven't, and they'll say I'm evil too, and they'll be back soon, and . . .'

There was evil here, sure enough. Or at least, there would be evil returning soon, when the parents came back . . .

'Mummy hid the key and I don't know where,' Susan mumbled. 'I tried to get Laura out, but I couldn't open the door on my own!'

'OK, OK.' Catherine gently pushed Susan away, then pressed her face to the cool wood of the cellar door. She raised her voice. 'Hello! Laura! Can you hear me?'

There was a long silence. All Catherine could hear was the blood pounding in her own head. The large house was silent – but somehow alive and watching her, waiting for her to do something.

Catherine called again. There was still no answer, but then, on the cusp of hearing, she could make out the faintest scratch. Was it someone moving about?

'I've got Susan here,' she called, 'and we're going to open the door, OK?'

She stepped back and studied the door. It looked solid. The keyhole was set below the doorknob; they both seemed to be part of the same mechanism, set into a metal plate. The plate was screwed into the door.

'Susan, do you know if there's a screwdriver anywhere?' she said. She was feeling more clear-headed now that she was actually doing something. It was just an empty house, no reason to be spooked.

Susan blinked at her, red eyed. 'I think there's one in the kitchen,' she said. She led Catherine back the way they had come and opened a drawer in the dresser. It was obviously the utilities drawer: Catherine spotted a hammer and some plugs and some fuses and an empty jam jar full of nails and, yes, a good, solid screwdriver. She took it out and hefted it in her hand.

They went back into the hall and Catherine kneeled down by the door. She wanted to keep talking to the little girl locked inside, letting her know that she wasn't on her own any more, that she would soon be safe.

'OK, Laura,' she called. 'I'm unscrewing the lock now.'

The screws had been in the wood a long time and had been painted over. Catherine had to gouge the dry, sticky paint out of the groove in each screw to get any kind of purchase. Her hands felt clammy on the screwdriver and she let go to wipe each one on her jeans. Out of the corner of her eye, she could see Susan hovering nearby, hopping from foot to foot.

Catherine tried again. The tip of the screwdriver slipped out with a jerk, making her gasp and leaving scratch marks down the door. She gritted her teeth and started again. This time the tip stayed put and the screw shifted. Catherine quickly pulled it out of the wood and gave it to Susan to hold. Then she turned her attention to the next.

There were four screws in all. Susan watched in silence while she removed each one. Then she jammed the screwdriver between the metal plate and the wood panel, and heaved. The plate prised slowly away from the door and left the lock mechanism exposed. Catherine had to unscrew that too, but it only took a minute. She levered it free and it fell to the floor with a metallic thud.

Catherine looked at the door and forced herself to take a deep breath. Laura could just be inches away on the other side. What exactly was she going to find when it opened? She really, *really* didn't want to go on.

But Susan needed her, not to mention Laura, so Catherine smiled bravely at the little girl. 'Almost there. Everything's going to be OK.'

She gave the door a push and it swung open on well-oiled hinges. Catherine leaned in. She could just make out the first couple of steps in a flight of wooden stairs leading down into the darkness.

'Hello?' she called softly. 'Laura? Don't be scared. I'm a friend of Susan's.'

She held her breath and waited for the tiny scratching sound she had heard before. There was still no answer, but it was definitely the sound of someone moving about.

'She won't come unless you go to her,' said Susan, and Catherine jumped. The little girl was standing right next to her, so close she could feel Susan's breath on her arm. 'She thinks our mum sent you.'

Catherine raised her eyebrows doubtfully, but Susan nodded. 'I know, because I'm her twin,' she explained.

Catherine looked around for a light switch, but couldn't see one.

'It's at the bottom,' Susan said.

'Oh, great.' Catherine looked into the darkness. Well, she had come this far. She couldn't leave now.

'OK, Laura, I'm coming down,' she called, and started to pick her way down the rickety wooden steps.

The air smelled of dust and damp. The steps creaked under her, but when she paused she thought she could hear whimpering, which spurred her on. She felt hard stone under her trainers and knew she'd reached the bottom of the stairs. She fumbled for the light switch on the wall and her fingers found it, but when she flicked it on, nothing happened. The light that came down from the hallway showed a small box of matches and the stub of a candle on a shelf next to the switch.

Catherine managed to light the candle on the third try, and a quivering triangle of yellow light stretched into the cellar.

The room was bare and empty, with walls that had once been painted white but now were covered with grime. At the far side, half engulfed in shadow, stood a little girl. Her clothes were tattered, her hair was matted and dirty, but her face was identical to Susan's. She was staring at Catherine with wide-eyed horror.

'Hello, Laura.' Catherine put all the warmth and encouragement she could into her voice. She took a step forward towards the other sister and Laura immediately took a step back. Catherine stopped moving.

'It's OK,' she soothed. 'I'm a friend of Susan's. I've come to get you out.'

Laura's chest started to heave. Her mouth moved but Catherine couldn't make out the words.

And then cold horror reached out with icy fingers and gripped Catherine by the throat. Just beyond

Laura, half hidden in the shadows on the floor, were two long, lumpy shapes. They looked like adults, sleeping . . .

Catherine strained her eyes as she peered into the gloom. She told herself it couldn't possibly be two people sleeping. She'd made enough noise breaking into the cellar to wake the dead . . . Except, of course, she hadn't. Because no amount of noise could wake the truly dead.

She had to get Laura out of here, and fast.

'Look,' she said. 'Susan's waiting upstairs. We can go up together and—'

Her eyes so huge that they seemed to swallow her whole face, Laura slowly raised one hand. Catherine stared in horror when she saw what was in it. An old-fashioned, dead-bolt key. The sort that would fit the cellar door.

'Is that the key . . .?' she began.

'*Why did you let her in?*' Laura screamed, making Catherine wince as her voice bounced around the walls. '*I thought I was safe down here!*'

Catherine frowned. 'What do you mean?' she asked, but Laura wasn't listening. She was staring at something just behind her. Catherine turned to see what it was.

Susan stood on the step just above her. Her face was a cold mask of hatred, and she was holding the kitchen knife Catherine had seen by the plate of sandwiches. The blade dripped red.

Susan lifted the knife, her fingers white where she clenched the handle. 'Thanks for everything, Catherine,' she whispered.

IS ANYBODY THERE?

Posters of the missing boy hung in a row at the back of the stage. Luke Benton was pleasant looking, blond, with a scattering of freckles. He wore a slightly bashful smile as if he couldn't quite believe he was being photographed. The picture that had been used for the posters was Luke's last school photo, taken the day he vanished. He had been wearing his school blazer and tie, and, though you couldn't see them in the picture, new black trainers with a silver trim. His entire outfit had been immortalized by the description on all the 'Missing: last seen wearing' posters that had been plastered around town.

Someone opened the door to the hall and the posters rustled in the breeze. Juliet Somerville made a mental note to stick them down at all four corners after the rehearsal. Luke's memorial service was going to be in two days' time, and having the posters waving about at the back of the stage would be distracting to everyone in the hall.

Juliet reckoned it would be quicker to do it herself than to mention it to Miss Worth. Their Head of Year could take the simplest idea and over-complicate it. She had already turned the rehearsal for the memorial into a three-ringed circus.

Privately, Juliet found it tasteless. Luke hadn't been seen for over a year. His phone hadn't been used, and no money had been taken out of his building society account. He had to be dead. He should be remembered in a church service or something, not a performance where people got stage fright and fretted about how they would look under the lights.

Miss Worth clapped her hands above the chatter in the hall until she had everyone's attention. 'Now, light desk – *light desk!* – thank you . . . and sound desk . . . both ready? Good. Now, can everyone who is going to read out a tribute to Luke form a queue on the left side of the stage . . . no, the *left* side . . . in alphabetical order of first name . . . or should that be order of age? Hmmm . . .'

Juliet nudged her best friend Christine. 'How about order of shoe size?' she whispered.

But Christine wasn't in a mood for jokes. 'Jules, I think Mark just looked at me!' she hissed. She stared across the hall. 'Look! He just did it again!'

Juliet followed her gaze, trying not to let her doubt show on her face. Mark Logan and his best friend Daniel Gardner were sitting together at the back of the hall. Mark had a stocky, powerful frame; Daniel was taller and darker, with a floppy fringe. Like most of the boys, they were in their football strip. All Luke's team-mates were going to wear their gear for the service as part of their tribute. If Mark had been looking at Christine, he wasn't now. He and Dan had their heads bowed together, deep in some private conversation.

'I wonder what they're talking about,' Christine breathed. 'I bet it's about Luke. Mark is such a deep thinker. He's so intellectual. He'll be sharing his thoughts about how loss and bereavement should make us appreciate the finer things of life, and draw us closer together in love.'

Juliet shot her friend a quick glance to check that she was being serious. Unfortunately, she was. 'Definitely that,' she agreed. 'Or, he scored a really cool goal in break and he's telling Daniel all about it.'

Christine scowled. 'You are such a cynic! They were Luke's closest friends, you know that.'

'So why didn't they volunteer to read tributes?' Juliet asked.

'Oh, Jules, you don't measure friendship like that!

Think about it. I mean, losing your best friend overnight – never even finding a body, just *losing* him – what must that be like? Of course they don't want to stand up in front of everyone. They probably haven't even begun to deal with what happened to Luke.'

'They could have got help, I don't know, some sort of counselling,' Juliet pointed out. She wasn't sure why; perhaps she just wanted to be stubborn, and to puncture Christine's inflated view of Mark. In the weeks after Luke's disappearance, the school had been overrun with well-meaning professionals urging his fellow students to put their emotions into words.

'And why should they? Why should they talk to some stranger about their inner feelings?' Christine's voice grew warm. 'They need someone who knows them, knows exactly what they're going through.'

In other words, Juliet thought, *they should talk to you!* But she didn't say it out loud. It would be mean – and maybe Christine could help the boys after all.

As the first anniversary of Luke's disappearance drew nearer, Mark and Daniel had become more and more withdrawn. If anyone approached them, even just brushed against them in the corridor, they could be snappish and irritable. So if Christine was able to help – well, good for her. She certainly couldn't do any harm.

Juliet looked down at the piece of paper in her hands. She had finished writing her tribute after a lot of crossing out and revision. *I first met Luke on our first day at this school, four years ago—*

Tears stung her eyes and she folded the paper up again. She would have to practise a lot more before she could stand up in front of everyone without losing it. She hadn't even known Luke that well, but she had liked the little she had seen of him. His sudden disappearance was so unnerving. And was he even, really, dead? He might have just run away! But everyone seemed to assume he *was* dead. There was all that talk about 'closure' – but how could you have closure when no one knew what had really happened to him? Something drifted into Juliet's mind, something about waters closing over your head, swallowing you up as if you'd never been there at all. That's what had happened to Luke. If it wasn't for the posters, she doubted that anyone would remember him at all. Even Mark and Daniel, who seemed most affected by his disappearance, never talked about him.

And that was why Juliet had decided to speak at the service. She wasn't going to drag up her doubts about him being dead – that would just be upsetting to everyone – but she would do everything she could to keep his *memory* alive.

Juliet pulled a face as she and Christine stepped out of the hall into the cold, grey winter evening. It was November and nights were long and icy. But the usual quantity of after-school chat hadn't changed, as boys and girls milled around waiting for the bus or a lift home. Others set off on their bikes, their red tail-lights wavering away into the gloom.

Juliet pulled her coat more firmly around her. She and Christine lived on opposite sides of town, so they would head in different directions once they reached the school gate.

'Talk to you later?' Juliet said.

'Yeah.' Christine shivered and tucked the ends of her scarf into her jacket. 'Give us a call.'

'Sure. Later.' They set off, walking quickly with their heads down against the wind.

Juliet had been at her school for four years, since she was eleven, but it was the first time she had done this particular walk in the dark. Her family had moved house over the summer. Daniel Gardner was her neighbour now; Luke's family lived three roads away on a slightly older part of the estate. As she turned off the main road, Juliet noticed with a small prickle of discomfort just how much difference a lack of light made. All the usual landmarks – a bent lamppost, the heavily graffitied bus shelter – only became visible close up. Everything seemed to take longer; all the distances seemed more drawn out.

This was the walk Luke would have made every day. And one day, he had set off, like her, into the darkness – and never been seen again.

'Oh, great,' Juliet muttered. 'I *so* needed to think about that.'

She turned right towards the park. Usually she walked straight across it. In the summer, there would be kids playing football or splashing each other by the fountain. Now, Juliet realized the park didn't have any lights. The road that ran around it was brightly lit but the large open stretch of grass and bushes in between looked like a gaping black hole. Juliet took one look and decided she would walk around the outside. It only added ten minutes to her journey.

Her heels clicked on the pavement and cars swished by on the road, little islands of warmth in the dusk. *Maybe I should start bringing my bike to school*, she thought. Put the lights on, stick to the main roads and still get home in half the time.

She came to Market Street on the far side of the

park. It wasn't much more than a narrow alley opposite the park's north entrance, leading to the main commercial part of town. Juliet peered unhappily down the alleyway. It was the only way to get through this block without adding another twenty minutes to her journey. At the other end, she could see the brightly lit market square, busy with people and buses. It wasn't far – just a minute away at a brisk pace. After that, she would be on the main road, with streetlights all the way to her front door. She started to walk.

The darkness seemed to swallow her up in just a few paces. Once her eyes adjusted, she could see details of the buildings on either side. The walls and doorways were pale, the windows into them black voids. Nearly all the buildings on this street had been vacant for some time now.

Juliet approached the old butcher's shop and shuddered. Huge metal doors had been nailed across the entrance to discourage squatters, and a large 'CONDEMNED' notice was plastered across them.

She could just make out the dark red paintwork and crumbling signs. The windows were veiled in dirt and cobwebs, and the shadows seem to cluster more thickly on the pavement outside.

To Juliet's surprise, there was a figure ahead, standing on tiptoes to peer into one of the grimy windows. Even though the light was very dim, Juliet recognized the tall, lanky frame, the mop of hair and the low-hanging fringe. It was Daniel.

She called into the darkness. 'Daniel? It's me – Juliet.'

Daniel spun round looking startled. 'I was . . . uh . . . checking for squatters,' he stammered. 'My dad owns this shop . . .'

'Squatters?' Juliet couldn't imagine anyone squatting somewhere so cold and uninviting. 'It doesn't look like anyone's got in, does it? It looks locked up for good.'

'Yeah . . . well . . .'

For a moment she thought their eyes might have met, but it was impossible to tell in the gloom. Then he brushed past her and headed back the way she had come, towards the park.

Juliet stood for a moment, watching his long-limbed silhouette trot into the light at the far end of the street. When his footsteps faded away, the street became abruptly quiet and cold again, its silence pressing down like an unwelcome fog. Suddenly Juliet felt like an intruder, a warm, live human in this cold, dead place. As she started to walk towards the market square, a shrill tune shattered the silence like ice.

Juliet jumped, then smiled, telling herself she'd let herself get spooked by the shadows. She fumbled to get her mobile phone out of her bag as she walked quickly towards the square. The little screen had lit up with an envelope icon and the words: '1 message received'.

She selected the 'read' command and stared at the 'sender' line. It wasn't from a number she recognized.

help me

Juliet scrolled down, but that was all there was.

Why would a stranger be asking for her help? Help me . . . do what?

Juliet selected 'reply'.

who r u? wots wrong?

She paused as she was about to hit 'send'. Maybe it was a marketing scam. If she replied to this number, she could be bombarded with texts about holidays in the sun or double-glazing or get-rich-quick schemes.

Or maybe it was someone who really needed help. So she pressed 'send', just as she came out into the busy, brightly lit market square.

The final stretch home was uphill, to where the new housing development sat in what had once been fields overlooking the town. Juliet's phone shrilled again as she reached her front door. The slog uphill had warmed her up, but she was looking forward to getting indoors and shutting out the cold, damp evening.

It was another text message.

Juliet clumsily turned the phone over in her gloved hands. The moment she stopped moving, a gust of frozen wind sliced right through her, doing nothing to improve her mood.

The message was from the same number.

im freezin

'Yeah, you and me both,' she muttered. Clearly she had a joker on her hands – some idiot who had got hold of her number and decided to have some fun. She dropped the phone back into her pocket and pushed her front door open.

'Hey, wasn't it about this time last year that that boy disappeared?' Juliet's father, never one to be up-to-the-minute, threw in the comment as the family were finishing dinner.

Juliet sighed. 'Yes, Dad,' she said. She had lost count of the times she had told him about the memorial service. It wasn't worth reminding him now.

'Must be hard for his parents,' he remarked, picking up the newspaper.

Juliet rolled her eyes, but her mother thought it a good time to chip into the conversation.

'You remember, Alan,' she said to Juliet's dad. 'The school's having that service in a couple of days. Juliet's doing a talk.'

'A reading, Mum,' Juliet corrected her.

'Really?' Her father looked at her over the paper. 'What about?'

'About Luke,' she muttered.

'Luke?'

'The boy who vanished!' Juliet just kept hold of her temper as she scraped up her last spoonful of cheesecake.

'Maybe we should run through whatever it is you're reading,' her dad continued. 'You do tend to swallow your consonants.'

'Dad, I spent all afternoon rehearsing! I don't need to go through it again!'

Her dad narrowed his eyes at her. 'There's no need to shout, young lady. Everyone needs to practise.'

'Leave the poor girl alone, Alan,' Juliet's mum put in. 'She's bound to be upset by this memorial service.'

'That doesn't excuse bad manners,' he said. 'This boy Luke – was he your boyfriend?'

'Alan, I think Juliet would have told us!' her mother exclaimed. She looked sideways at her. 'Wouldn't you? He *wasn't* your boyfriend, was he?'

'Mum, I hardly knew him,' Juliet muttered.

'Fair enough, dear. But I'm very pleased to hear from Christine that the two of you are going around with Daniel and Mark. It will do you all good.'

'*What?*' Juliet said. This was the first she had heard of it! She would throttle Christine, and smile while she did it.

'Well, I talked to Christine earlier and . . . oh,

sorry, wasn't I meant to know?' Her mother winked. 'Is it a *secret?*'

Juliet buried her face in her hands, and left the table to go upstairs as soon as she could without being snapped at.

'Practise that speech!' her father called after her.

Later that night Juliet lay in bed with the light out, looking up at the ceiling. She had spent the evening staring at her maths homework. Usually it all made sense – in fact maths was one of her strongest subjects – but tonight the equations had just been so many squiggles on the paper. Her mind was running in too many different directions to think about the value of x or y. Luke, death, Dad being annoying . . .

And thanks to her best friend, her mum was convinced she had a new boyfriend.

'God, you're for it, Chris,' she mumbled, just as her phone went off with another message tone. She fumbled around on her bedside table and the display on her phone lit up, throwing a ghostly glow around the room.

It was the same number as before.

i cant get out

Juliet groaned. Who was this jerk?

She stopped for a second.

Suppose someone really did need her help? OK, it was someone who only bothered to send texts every few hours, so they couldn't be in *that* much trouble – whatever the problem was, it was obviously taking its time to reach a critical moment – but even so . . .

She sat up in bed. She would call this idiot and find out. If he really was in trouble, she would see what she could do. And if it was just someone messing around, he – or she – would be *very* sorry.

Juliet selected 'call back' and held the phone to her ear. While the call connected, there was nothing but the sound of her own heartbeat echoing off the phone and back into her head.

Suddenly the phone shrilled three notes into her ear and a polite voice said: '*Sorry, the number you have dialled has not been recognized. Please check and try again.*'

'What do you mean?' Juliet said out loud, though she knew it was only a recording. 'That's impossible!' How could the number not be recognized? She couldn't be getting messages from a number that didn't exist!

She knew how you could do that with email – fake the headers in a message so that it appeared to come from somewhere else. But she hadn't heard of it being done with a text.

But if someone was doing it deliberately, at least that meant they couldn't be in trouble. They were just doing it to wind her up, and she wasn't going to give them the satisfaction of knowing they'd got to her. She pressed the 'off' key with her thumb, and held it down until the phone went dead.

* * *

Juliet woke up feeling quite well rested, despite dreaming about equations. The other things that had been bothering her the night before seemed very distant. She felt for the light switch and screwed up her eyes before turning it on.

Her phone lay where she had left it on her bedside table, its blank, grey screen staring up. She turned it back on. While the screen went through its wake-up process, she put it down again and headed for the bathroom.

The message tune played before she reached the door.

Juliet stopped. She turned and looked at the phone. Uncertainty tugged at the back of her mind. Was it another of those dumb messages? She turned round and crossed the room in two steps. Snatching the phone up, she checked the message screen. She was going to give this creep *such* a . . .

The message was from Christine. It had been sent last night, after Juliet had turned her phone off.

'Oh – Chris!' Juliet breathed in relief.

hi j! wanna come to high st rftr school 2 hit the shops?

Shopping with Christine suddenly seemed like the best thing she could think of to take her mind off the idiot that kept texting her. Juliet grinned as she sent back:

Sure! cu l8r

The phone beeped again almost immediately, and she smiled as she glanced down at the screen. Christine was obviously in need of some serious retail therapy! Then she read:

im scared

'Dad?' Juliet said at breakfast.

'Hmm?' he said absently, stabbing his knife into the marmalade while flattening the newspaper with his other hand.

While she was getting dressed, Juliet had thought long and hard over telling her dad about the messages. If he thought they were nothing to worry about, he would say so. But if she was being stalked by some anonymous weirdo, surely he'd want to know? So she said, tentatively, 'I've been getting these text messages . . .'

'That's nice.'

His absent-mindedness was annoying and it gave Juliet more courage to speak. 'No, it's not. They're creepy.' She held the phone up and scrolled through them. 'They're all from someone I don't know. Look. *Help me. I'm freezin. I can't get out. I'm scared.* Dad, they're . . . well, they're creepy.'

'Yes, it's probably . . .' His voice trailed away as a headline caught his eyes. 'Oh, for crying out loud! Can't one day go by without people speculating about property prices? People shouldn't overstretch themselves with their mortgages, that would stop all this nonsense.'

'Dad!' Juliet protested.

'Sorry, love.' He barely lifted his eyes from the page. 'Yes, probably just some silly boy with a crush on you, trying to get your attention. Ignore him . . . Honestly! Up another one per cent?'

'I'm going to school,' Juliet muttered.

She stomped down the hill in a foul mood. She now had four messages on her phone from a number that didn't exist, and whoever was at the other end either had a sick sense of humour or needed her help badly.

The weather did nothing for her mood. It was warmer than yesterday, but made up for that with a very fine drizzle. The water seemed to hang in the air, and you only knew it was there when it had soaked you. By the time Juliet reached the bottom of the hill, she knew she was going to arrive at school dripping wet.

But, slowly, something penetrated her bad temper – an awareness that she was not alone. She was being followed by a car – a car that was slowly pursuing her down the road and exactly matching her pace.

She was in no mood for this at all. Deciding that she probably wasn't about to be abducted in broad daylight, she stopped with her hands on her hips and glared straight at the windscreen. The car was a brand-new, metallic blue roadster, its windows misted with fine drops of water.

The driver's window slid down and a young man peered out. 'Hey, Jules!'

Juliet relaxed at once. 'Dave!' She looked quickly from left to right, then darted across the road.

Dave was her cousin. He was only a few years older than her, close enough to be more like her big brother, especially as she didn't have any real brothers or sisters.

'Drive you to school?' Dave offered.

Juliet grinned. 'Sure!'

She ran round to the passenger door and climbed in. Inside it was warm and dry, and had that sort of shiny plastic smell of new cars.

'Very nice,' she said approvingly as she looked

around the spotless interior. 'How long have you had it?'

'Picked it up on Friday,' Dave said proudly. 'I've got a pay review coming up so I thought I'd celebrate.'

'That's great,' she said. 'They must like you at the station!' Dave was a police constable. He was wearing part of his uniform now – he had his own leather jacket on, but underneath she could see the collar of his white shirt done up with a dark tie, and dark blue trousers.

Maybe she shouldn't write her entire family off as useless, Juliet thought. 'Dave,' she began slowly, 'can I ask you something?'

Dave listened carefully as she told him about the messages. When she had finished, his face was stern. 'Jules, if you're being harassed then you have to report it! Tell the phone company. They can cut the guy off if they have to.'

'But the number doesn't exist!' she reminded him.

'It exists, or it wouldn't be calling you. It's called

spoofing, Jules – it's perfectly possible to disguise the identity of a mobile phone. It just takes a bit of extra know-how. I'd be surprised if the company can't track it.'

Juliet paused, turning her phone over in her hands. She wanted to ask Dave a really big favour. 'Could *you* track it? I mean, if I didn't make this a formal report – could you do it, just between the two of us?'

Dave looked at her for a moment, then turned back to the road. 'Well, I could,' he said. 'But we get into all kinds of trouble if we use police resources for our own purposes. Unless you actually want to report this guy, Jules, it's not police business.'

'But I don't want to report him – whoever it is,' Juliet said helplessly. 'That's why I'm asking you like this. I'm afraid of overreacting. If it's a sick stalker then yeah, sure, I'd want to report him, but if it's just some dumb kid at school who thinks he's funny, he wouldn't be worth making a fuss about. And if it's someone in trouble, well, I want to help him. But I don't know which it is! And I won't know unless I know where the number comes from.' She broke off in confusion.

They had reached the school gates and Dave pulled over. 'Can I see these messages, Jules?'

She handed him her phone and watched him scroll through the texts. He raised his eyebrows as he read each one under his breath.

Suddenly Juliet gasped and gripped the edge of her seat. A vision had hit her, an absolute certainty about the stranger at the other end of the line. It was someone alone, and cold, and scared. And in the dark. A small, dark, closed space. He was hardly able to breathe . . .

Juliet bit her lip. Where had all that come from? There was no way she could know all that just from a few dumb texts. It was just someone messing around, right?

Dave was looking at her, concerned. 'It's really getting to you, isn't it?' he said softly. She nodded, not trusting herself to speak. He sighed and handed the phone back.

'Write the number down,' he said, 'and I'll see what I can do.'

Juliet felt slightly better as she walked into the school. Maybe by the end of the day Dave would have told her who had made the calls and she'd be able to confront them. She couldn't wait to see the look on their face.

Christine ambushed her just inside the gate. 'Jules! Jules! It's *so* cool!' Juliet let herself be dragged over to the edge of the playground. Christine's eyes were shining and there were spots of bright colour on her cheeks.

'Mark said he'd go out with me! With *me*! And he's going to meet us in the high street this afternoon.'

'Us?' Juliet echoed.

'Of course, us! You said you'd come, remember?'

Juliet had completely forgotten about fixing up to go shopping after school. Talking to Dave, and her worries about the stranger, had driven it out of her mind, even though she had really liked the idea when Christine first texted it. But Christine plus Mark mooning over each other was the last thing she wanted. She wondered if she'd be able to find an excuse to get out of it before the end of the day – maybe Dave calling her with the stalker's identity.

'Sure,' she replied.

The day dragged by and Juliet's mood dragged with it. In the lunch break, her phone went off – but this time it was the usual ring tone. Someone was calling her, not texting, but she wasn't reassured when she looked at the screen and saw 'Number withheld'.

'Hey, you going to answer that?' Christine asked, and Juliet realized she had been standing with the phone in her hand, staring at it.

'Um, yeah, of course,' she said. She pressed the green talk key and carefully held it to her ear. 'H-hello?'

'You sound totally spooked,' said a man's voice. 'Are you OK?'

Juliet breathed out in relief. 'Hi, Dave. Yeah, I . . .' She wasn't sure what to say.

'Jules, I did some finding out about that, uh, thing you asked me to find out,' he said.

Juliet's heart started to pound and her fingers felt slippery against the phone. 'Yes?'

Dave sighed. 'Your spoofer is better than I thought. He's using a number that's been out of use for a year. It was last used one year ago tomorrow, in fact.'

'Who by?' Juliet wanted to know.

'Sorry, Jules, that's personal information and I really can't hand it out. Look, take this to the phone company. That's the best thing you can do. Bye.'

Juliet stared at the phone in frustration as the line disconnected. It sounded like Dave was convinced this was the work of a joker, using a dead number. But what was the point of this joke? If someone was trying to freak her out, wouldn't it be better to call her? Maybe breathe heavily, try and get her to say something? Wouldn't they want to hear how she sounded?

'Right,' she murmured. She was going to get to the bottom of this. The surest way to be spooked was to *let* herself be spooked. But she could fight back instead. Confront him – whoever he was. Or she.

She selected the last message received, then thumbed 'reply' and sent back:

> *i dont know who u r but i cant help if u dont tell me wots going on*

The envelope icon spun around on the screen and the display read 'Message delivered'. Almost immediately it switched to 'Message received', and the phone buzzed in her hand.

Juliet blinked in surprise and selected the new message.

> *im ya friend i need u*

Juliet almost dropped the phone. No way, *no way* could someone have had time to tap in a reply to her text. No way!

But someone had.

The shops were busy and lit with garish lights. It was mid-November and they were already steaming towards Christmas with decoration-overload and a constant background of cheesy Christmas songs. There were three levels inside the shopping centre and Christine and Juliet headed straight for the second floor, where all the best clothes shops were.

'Chris,' Juliet said as they rode up the escalator.

Christine rubbed a stick of gloss over her lips. The fake strawberry scent made Juliet feel a bit sick. 'Hmmm?'

'Um, what would you do if you had, um, a stalker?'

Christine twisted the lip-gloss back into its tube and dropped it into her handbag. 'I don't know. Depends who, I suppose.'

'Suppose you didn't know? Suppose he just had

your phone number and kept sending you weird messages?'

Christine grinned. 'That would be even cooler! I could imagine who it was and I'd never be disappointed.'

Juliet suspected Christine wasn't the right person to expect any sympathy from, especially when it felt weird telling her about the messages in the first place. 'But—' she began.

'Look!' Christine gasped. They had reached the top of the elevator. Christine clutched Juliet's arm and dragged her in through the door of the nearest shop. 'You've got to help me,' she insisted. 'There are these two tops and they are both *so* cool, but I need to know which one Mark will like most . . . Wait there.'

She dropped Juliet's arm and vanished between the racks of clothes, leaving Juliet to fume silently. Weren't friends meant to talk to each other? How could you when one of them wouldn't listen to anything important?

She took out her phone and gazed at it as if it held the secret of the mysterious caller, and all she had to do was stare it down until it revealed his identity. She scrolled idly through the messages, until the last one appeared on the screen . . .

Suddenly the phone was snatched out of her hand.

'Jules! Really!' Christine was back – how long had she been there? – clutching a pair of tops on hangers. 'Pay attention, please! This is so much more important than . . .' She glanced at the message, and her eyes went round.

'Oh my God! Oh my *God!*' For a moment, Juliet thought her friend was being freaked out by the creepy messages – and oddly, this made her feel better. Maybe she wasn't overreacting after all.

But then Christine dropped her voice and looked from side to side, as if checking they weren't being overheard. 'So this is what you meant about text messages! You've got a *boyfriend!* Why didn't you *say?*'

Juliet snatched the phone back. 'I have not got

a boyfriend!' she hissed. 'I don't know who it is. Someone's been sending me all these anonymous texts and—'

Christine drew in her breath sharply. Her hand flew to her mouth, smudging her carefully applied lip-gloss. 'Wait, Jules! I know exactly who it is!'

'Who?' Juliet was ready to listen to any theory.

'It's *Daniel*! Come on, you know it makes sense! We're best friends, aren't we? And Mark and Daniel are best friends, so of course he wants to go out with you! He's trying to get a date!'

'By stalking me anonymously?' Juliet muttered, but Christine wasn't listening.

'Oh, Jules, the four of us together! This is so *fantastic*!' She pulled Juliet into a hug. 'Look, let's forget these stupid tops. Let's go and meet Mark right now. I told him you'd be here this afternoon. I'll bet you anything Daniel's with him.'

Juliet doubted it, but she let Christine pull her out of the shop. She couldn't recall Daniel ever showing the slightest sign of interest in her. If he *was* trying to ask her out . . . well, she had to admit that, yes, the four of them together did have a nice sound to it. Daniel had quite a nice smile, the few times he bothered to show it. Kind of shy, suggesting there was more to the joke that he'd like to share with you.

And if Daniel *was* sending the messages — well, that would be about a billion times less scary, because she would have no difficulty confronting him about it. She could make a joke out of it, tell him there were much better ways to get her attention, like cinema trips and skipping Games on a Friday afternoon to hang out.

But she didn't think it was him, and not just because Christine's logic was based more on hope than fact. Daniel had looked straight through her when they had passed outside the butcher's shop — in fact, hadn't he been running away from her when the first text arrived a few seconds later? He hadn't shown the slightest sign of being interested in her then, and he couldn't have sent a text while he was belting down the alley towards the park. No, Juliet didn't believe Daniel was the one.

Whoever was texting her was still out there – but where?

One of Christine's predictions turned out to be true, however: Daniel was with Mark when they met up. The boys had already staked out a table at the Coffee Place. Mark stood up with a smile when he saw them coming.

'Hi, Chris,' he said. There was a warmth there which was at odds with Juliet's impression of him so far – withdrawn and reserved, and impatient with people he didn't know very well. Maybe he really did care for Christine, and maybe she really was helping him get over the Luke thing. If so, Juliet was glad.

'Hi,' Christine gasped, and she clutched at Juliet's arm for a moment. Juliet tried not to wince.

Daniel followed Mark's lead more slowly, his gangly frame unfolding from his chair. He looked at

Juliet and she was *almost* certain Christine was wrong about his feelings. Daniel's fringe hid his eyes, and it was hard to tell what he was thinking, but the set of his mouth didn't show much enthusiasm.

'Hey, Juliet,' he said flatly.

'Hey,' she replied, equally flatly.

If he was going to be *that* uninterested, she realized, he probably wasn't going to offer drinks, and she was thirsty.

'Can we get you something?' she said pointedly.

He shrugged. 'Sure. Coke.'

'Yeah, that would be good,' Mark added.

'OK,' Christine said. She looked deliriously happy at the privilege of getting a drink for her boyfriend. 'Ice? Slice of lemon?'

Slice of lemon? In this place? They'd be lucky. 'Come on, Chris, we haven't got all day,' Juliet muttered, dragging her over to the counter.

The girl behind the counter seemed determined to break records for slow service. It would have been just as quick to wait for her to grow a couple of lemon trees out the back. Christine took the first two Cokes back to the table, and Juliet had to wait a couple more minutes for the next two. When she got back to the others, her heart plummeted as she heard what Christine was chatting about.

'. . . some secret admirer, *texting* her all the time . . .'

The way Christine said it, and the way she was looking at Daniel out of the corner of her eye, showed exactly who she thought was sending the messages. Daniel just looked bored.

'Chris, it's not a big deal . . .' Juliet began.

'Not a big deal?' Christine protested. 'Come on!'

Before Juliet could stop her, Christine yanked her phone from her bag, called up the messages menu and thrust it into Daniel's face. Juliet's hands were full of Coke glasses and she could only watch helplessly in dismay.

'So, what do you make of that, hey, Daniel?' Christine demanded.

Daniel took the phone and looked at the screen.

His face went white and he slammed the phone down on the table as if it had burned his hands.

'Got a problem, Danno?' Mark said. He picked the phone up and looked casually at the screen. 'Ah, it's nothing. Just some stupid marketing thing. They send stuff like this all the time, and charge you loads for replying. Forget it, Juliet. I've heard there are phones now that can block numbers you don't want to call you. Maybe you should get one? Don't you think, Dan?' He looked hard at his friend, and Daniel flushed.

'Uh, yeah,' he said. 'Good idea.'

'Yeah,' Juliet muttered. 'Maybe.' She remembered she had thought it might be a marketing hoax, the very first time she got a message. But since then she had had that talk with Dave, and learned about the old number. Surely a marketing company would use a new number?

Daniel twitched back his sleeve and looked at his watch. 'Hey, I've, uh, gotta go,' he said. 'Got . . . uh

. . . something.' He pushed back his chair and smiled weakly at Juliet. 'Sorry.'

Mark frowned. 'I thought we were going to the movie?'

'Yeah, well, you know . . .' Daniel said vaguely. He was already backing away. As soon as he reached the door of the café he turned and vanished into the crowds of shoppers.

Christine turned to Juliet, her eyes round with distress. 'Oh, Jules, I'm so sorry! I didn't think he'd stand you up like that. That guy is such an idiot . . .'

'Stand you up?' said Mark. 'Has Dan asked you out or something?'

'Oh, come on,' Christine said before Juliet could reply. 'You just have to look at him . . .'

'It's nothing,' Juliet put in. 'Really, it's nothing.'

'Yeah, well, fancy technology always did freak Gardner out,' Mark said, waving Juliet's phone. 'This must have scared him away. Dan likes to live in the Stone Age. He doesn't even have one of these.'

'*What?*' Christine couldn't have sounded more

shocked if she had just learned Daniel lived in a cardboard box. 'He doesn't have a mobile phone!'

Juliet stared at Mark, gripping the edge of the table. 'Are you sure about that? That he doesn't have a phone, I mean?'

'Nah, he can't stand them,' Mark said casually. He sipped his Coke. 'It really winds me up when we're trying to fix football practice.'

Juliet's mind was reeling. Even though she had been fairly sure it wasn't Daniel sending her the messages, the fact that he didn't have a mobile meant it definitely wasn't. And right now, she wasn't sure how she felt about that. The idea of a truly anonymous stalker suddenly seemed even more threatening than before, and she wanted to get out of the stuffy café and find somewhere quieter to think. 'Can I have my phone back, Mark?' she asked.

'Hmm?' Mark realized he was still holding her phone. 'Oh, yeah, sure. Sorry.'

He handed it back and Juliet shoved it into her bag. Then she pushed back her chair and practically ran out of the café, trying not to think that anyone could be sending the texts – maybe even someone in the shopping centre, someone watching her right now, waiting for her to be alone . . .

The murmur of the full school hall came through the thick stage curtains. Miss Worth was in organizing overdrive, her glasses shoved into her wiry hair as she co-ordinated Juliet and Christine and Mark and Daniel and everyone else who would be taking part in the memorial service. Today was The Day – exactly 365 days after Luke Benton's disappearance.

Juliet ran through her lines under her breath one more time. Christine had said she could read them out to her for practice . . . but of course, Christine was on the other side of the stage, with Mark, looking completely out of place among the football team.

On an impulse, Juliet pulled her phone from her pocket. She opened up a blank message and texted *hey, rmbr me?* She selected Christine's number and pressed 'send'.

The phone vibrated in her hand – Miss Worth had told everyone to turn their phones off, and Juliet had compromised by setting it to silent mode. She frowned at the screen. The dialogue box read 'Unable to send message' and showed a bulging envelope icon. She groaned. This happened when the inbox and outbox filled up with stored messages. It meant she would have to go through all her old texts and decide which ones to keep, and which to delete. She knew she could just select 'delete all' and empty her phone right out – but some of the old messages had sentimental value and she wanted to keep them a bit longer. The text Christine had sent her to cheer her up when she got a detention, for example, or the one from her cousin Dave announcing his engagement.

There were still several minutes before the start of the memorial service. Juliet ducked her head and started to delete the routine messages – the arrangements with Christine to meet up after school, sharing gossip, checking on homework. That bit was easy. But then she came to the five anonymous messages, and realized she wasn't sure if she wanted to keep them or not. She moved the cursor idly up and down the list, looking at the brief, almost meaningless words, and the dates and times each message had been sent.

Then something odd struck her. She knew the most recent message had come in yesterday, and the first had arrived two days ago. But all the messages appeared to have been sent on the same day. And it was *today's* date.

For a moment, she wondered if something was wrong with her phone's SIM card. She scrolled down to a different message, the one Christine had sent her about going shopping. No, that had the right date attached to it, two days ago. Juliet went back to the five anonymous messages.

There was something else odd about the dates. The day and the month were the same as today . . .

but the year was different. The messages were dated from this exact day one year before.

Today, the anniversary of Luke Benton's disappearance, was also the anniversary of these texts being sent!

Even stranger, now that Juliet was in the mood to notice things, was the *times* the messages seemed to have been written. They had been sent to her in reverse order, each one written a few minutes earlier than the one before. The last message she had got, *im ya friend*, was the first to be texted. If you put them into the right order, they read like this:

im ya friend i need u
im scared
i cant get out
im freezin
help me

Juliet felt icy fingers run down her spine and she shivered, even though it was hot and stuffy behind the curtains. She stared at the tiny screen, trying to make some sense – any sense – out of what she read, and she almost dropped the phone as another message came in and it vibrated like an insect in her palm. She checked the screen and bit back a sob.

'Oh no,' she whispered. 'Oh no, oh please, just go away.'

It was from the same number as before, and it had been sent before any of the others.

the place is locked up for good

'What place?' Juliet murmured. She shut her eyes, putting all the clues together. It was freezing, it was locked up – she had that flash again of somewhere cold, dark and airless, so hard to breathe . . . She shivered and thrust the phone back into her pocket. Where had all this stuff come from? This was really starting to get to her, worming its way into her thoughts . . .

Something to do with the last message rang a

small bell in her mind. Something about being locked up for good . . .

Market Street, she thought, and shuddered again. For a moment it was as if she was back there on that cold, damp evening two nights ago. Halfway along Market Street, outside the deserted butcher's shop; Daniel looking through the filthy window, apparently checking for squatters.

'It looks locked up for good,' she had said.

It had only been a few moments after that when the first message came in.

Juliet folded her fingers around the phone in her pocket. Somehow, the deserted butcher's shop was connected with this.

'Hey, Jules, where are you going?'

Christine's voice was muffled by the damp evening mist, and Juliet pretended not to hear as she scooted out of the school gates. She had slipped out of the hall as soon as the service was over, and now she stuffed her hands in her pockets and walked quickly down the road. For a moment she felt guilty for avoiding Christine like this. But then she reminded herself that Christine just didn't – couldn't – understand how creeped out Juliet was about these messages, and it would take too long to explain. This was something Juliet had to do on her own.

She walked on into the dark.

A cold wind was blowing down Market Street, and the dank gloom of the narrow lane only made it seem colder, even more like a scene from an old black and white movie.

The butcher's shop had been little more than a black shape the last time Juliet saw it, its windows dark holes into the unknown. Now that she could see it more clearly, in the reddening twilight, it looked even more menacing. It was square and blocky and ugly. Its paint seemed deliberately tattered, as if it had never been smart, even when it was first painted. It was like the kid in school who sits through lessons with his feet up on the desk.

Juliet didn't jump when her phone shattered the

quiet with its message tone. She had almost expected it to. She checked what had come in.

i fink they all went home

Juliet shuddered. Whoever had sent this was all alone – just like she was now.

'I wish I was at home too,' she muttered.

She pressed her face to the window. The grimy glass reflected her own face back at her, a pale pinkish smudge against the grey, and she could see nothing bar a few hard-edged shapes inside. The bottom of the pane was smeared with handmarks; she wondered if they belonged to Daniel, from when he had been peering in. Juliet wondered why his dad hadn't organized proper security if he was so concerned about squatters.

She stepped back from the shop and gazed up at its decaying front.

'Just what am I doing here?' she wondered out loud. Surely it was just coincidence that this was where she'd received the first anonymous text?

'Ah, forget it,' she muttered. 'Get a grip, Jules.'

She turned to go, and her phone sounded.

Juliet stopped dead. What were the chances, she thought bitterly, that Christine was texting her to say she had split up with Mark?

Very faint, she knew as she pulled the phone out. Very faint indeed.

It wasn't Christine, it was the year-old number.

they locked me in

Juliet's breath caught in her throat. Locked in! It doubled the horror of the vision she'd had before. If she'd thought about it at all, she'd somehow assumed the person had ended up in the freezing, dark, airless room by accident. That was bad enough.

Had they been locked in *deliberately*?

Juliet scanned the sheets of metal nailed over the front of the shop. Not even a door handle showed. She looked around and saw the dark slit of a narrow passageway running between this shop and the next one. The front door was boarded up but there had to be a back one.

 i cant get out . . .

Juliet inched down the passageway, turning sideways when her feet squelched in something she didn't want to inspect too closely. Her shins connected hard with what felt like a dustbin and she cursed under her breath, then louder when she realized there was no one to hear her. At last the walls of the passageway fell away on either side, and she stumbled into the yard at the back of the shop.

It was enclosed by high brick walls, topped with rusty barbed wire and broken glass. From the piles of rubbish shoved against the edges, with shadows that seemed to shift and blur in the gloom, it looked like the whole street dumped its junk here. But sure enough, there was a door into the back of the old butcher's shop, and it didn't seem to have been boarded up.

Juliet put her hand on the handle and pushed, then shook it. Not boarded, but still locked fast with a new and strong-looking padlock just above the handle. She could also see the smooth round eye of a conventional Yale lock. There was a window in the top half of the door, with a blind pulled down inside to hide the shop from view. The window was covered by a metal grille attached to the outside, reddish with rust and twisting away from the wooden frame at one corner.

im ya friend i need u

Juliet stepped back and her foot knocked into something that gave a metallic clink. She had dislodged a small heap of metal pipes, stacked against a battered china sink. She bent down and wrapped her hands around a cold, heavy length of pipe. She slid one end into the loop of the padlock and pushed down as hard as she could. The clasp bent slowly at first, then broke open with a jerk.

That leaves the Yale lock, Juliet thought. She'd have to smash the window and reach in to open it from the inside. She threaded her fingers into the grille and tugged. She felt something shift, but after that the grille held fast. She picked up the pipe again and jammed it carefully between the door and the grille. The grille lifted away from the woodwork, its screws tearing free with a splintering crack. It came away more quickly than Juliet was expecting, and her knuckles banged into the rough brick wall. She put her hand in her mouth to suck the graze. Now she just had to break the window, and she'd be in.

She swung the pipe and tried not to feel too satisfied when the glass shattered. She reached gingerly in through the hole, being careful not to cut herself on the jagged glass stuck in the frame. Something cold and damp brushed against her fingers and she almost screamed, until she realized it was only the blind inside the door.

i fink they all went home

Her fingers found the latch of the lock, though she had to stand at an odd, shoulder-straining angle to reach it. She took a firm grip and twisted. The latch gave way with a rusty snap. She put her shoulder against the frame and pushed. It slowly, grudgingly swung open. Just as slowly, Juliet sidled into the cold, dark building.

the place is locked up for good

The shop smelled of dust and mould. At first, all she could see were vague, squarish shapes and more pools of shadow. She instinctively fumbled for the light switch beside the door, and stifled a shriek as she thrust her fingers into a mass of cobwebs. She pulled her hand back and wiped it against her coat.

By now, her eyes were adjusting to the dark. All the furniture, desks, anything that might have given a clue to what this room was before, had been taken away. The floor had a pattern of checked tiles, squares of dark and light grey that might have been white once upon a time.

Juliet took a step forward. She could hear something small moving around by her foot, something that skittered and was very much alive. She sprang backwards and bumped into the wall, dislodging a small cloud of grit that fell into her hair. She brushed her hands frantically over her head while the small, dark shape — a mouse? a rat? — scuttled across the floor. It vanished into a hole in the wall on her right.

Juliet made herself take deep, steady breaths until she felt her pounding heart slow down. She looked around. There was a door straight in front of her that must lead to the main part of the shop. Another door on her right stood half open, and she could just make out a flight of stairs beyond.

help me

There was a third door in the far left-hand corner of the room.

It took a moment for Juliet to realize it was a door at all because it was taller and wider than the others. At first she thought it was just a bit of wall that was painted differently. Now her eyes had adjusted, she could see what it was more clearly. It was darker than the wall next to it, and it gleamed metallically in the orange light that filtered from the boarded-up windows in the front of the shop.

Juliet didn't know much about how a butcher's shop was run, but she knew there must have been somewhere to keep the meat. Somewhere bigger than your typical fridge. This must have been the butcher's cold store.

im freezin

She walked cautiously up to the door and ran her fingers over the brushed metal surface. There was a long, vertical handle at waist height. Knobs and dials were set into a panel on the wall next to it, which presumably had once set the temperature. They were all dead now, of course, the power long cut off.

they locked me in

The door was like the entrance to a bank vault. If anyone had been locked in somewhere in this building, this would be it. Any other room, you only had to knock the door down, or climb out of a window. But someone locked in here . . . What chance would they have of getting out?

And did that mean Juliet really wanted to see what was on the other side?

She shuddered, but she took hold of the handle in both hands. She had come this far. She had to know.

She let go of the handle again. She *didn't* want to know. She wanted to go home, right now.

they locked me in

A sob broke out of her as she stood still, trembling.

im scared

With a wordless shout of anger and fear, she gripped the lever and pulled. It didn't shift. She took hold of it again, braced her feet on the slippery floor and heaved, grunting with the effort. Did it budge slightly? She braced again and threw herself backwards, yanking on the lever as hard as she could.

Something clicked, and the door moved a couple of centimetres.

Juliet still needed both hands on the lever, but slowly the door opened. A blast of ancient air hit her full in the face, followed immediately by a stench so horrible, so evil, that it made her gag. It was dead and rotting. It was everything that should not be.

they locked me in

Juliet staggered back with her sleeve over her mouth. Someone must have left some old meat hung up in there. It was the worst thing she had ever smelled.

She held her breath and took a step forward to peer into the storage room, but the space inside could have been as small as a phone box or as big as a football stadium for all she could see. The shadows inside seemed blacker and thicker than anywhere else, swallowing all the feeble light that penetrated the rest of the room. Juliet waited for her stomach to stop heaving, then pulled the door open as far as it would go to let the light in.

help me

The shadows slid back enough for Juliet to see that the room was a steel-lined cube. The walls were sheer and smooth, and curved steel hooks dangled from racks on the ceiling. Sides of beef and bacon had once hung from them, but now they just swayed a little in the slight breeze that Juliet had caused. And the floor . . .

The floor was smooth with white ceramic tiles. The stale, dusty orange light edged across it as the door opened, trickling over a pair of shoes lying in the far corner.

Trainers – black with a silver trim.

Juliet pushed the door open the last few centimetres. The band of light shifted to reveal a pair of legs in dark trousers. Then the rest of the body. And the head.

The body was slumped against the wall, as if it had been sitting up when it died. Juliet recognized the school blazer, but she could have guessed who it was anyway.

She had found Luke Benton.

The skin was drawn tight over the hands, the outlines of the bones strained against it as if ready to burst out. Juliet bent down and forced herself to look at the face. Luke's eyes had shrunk to dark pits. His lips were drawn back and his teeth were bared as if he was grinning with desperate humour. His cheekbones stood out in sharp relief. It made Juliet think of images of Egyptian mummies.

One of Luke's hands was folded across his lap, the other lay beside him on the floor, palm up, his fingers curled around a mobile phone.

Juliet craned her neck, trying to see the screen of the phone without getting closer to the body – to Luke. The angle was too awkward, she had no choice but to reach out and pluck it gently from his hand, using just two fingers, straining not to have any contact with Luke's dead flesh. His fingers gripped the phone tighter than she had thought, and for a moment, as she lifted it, his hand rose too. Juliet clenched her teeth so hard that her eyes hurt. Suddenly his lifeless grasp gave way and his hand flopped back on to the tiled floor.

Juliet turned the phone towards the light. She was familiar with the model – she had the same one – and she knew how to turn it on, but nothing happened when she held the key down. The battery had died long ago.

But there was one thing she could do. She quickly opened the phone up, pulled out the SIM card and swapped it with her own. She turned her phone on again, and the screen lit up with Luke's last messages.

There they were, in the outbox. All of them, in the order he had sent them – the reverse of the order she had received them.

they locked me in
i fink they all went home . . .

None of them were listed as sent. Juliet scrolled through the last message until she came to the message report. She flicked through the date and time of sending until she came to the final line: 'Error: unable to send msg'.

'Oh, Luke,' she murmured, as her eyes filled with tears. 'I'll get you out of here. I'll go and get help . . .'

'Be quiet!'

'I'm trying!'

Juliet spun round. Someone else had entered the room at the back of the shop; two voices, two sets of footsteps shuffling over the tiled floor. Instinct made Juliet move to one side, out of the cone of light that fell in through the open door. She stood pressed against the wall. She couldn't see who was there, but that meant they couldn't see her either.

'Look, we don't know someone's been in here . . .'

'That door had been forced open!'

'OK, Danno, OK . . .'

Danno! Juliet shut her eyes and breathed out slowly in relief. She recognized the voices now. It was only Daniel, still worried about squatters in his dad's shop, and he had brought Mark along for support.

She opened her eyes, and saw the cone of light shrinking across the floor of the cold store. She stepped away from the wall just in time to see the smooth steel door swinging shut.

Juliet screamed and ran at it. It closed and the light vanished at the same moment as she crashed against the metal.

'STOP! Open this door!' she shrieked. She dropped the phone and scrabbled blindly at the smooth, steel surface. *'Wait! Open the door! Daniel! Mark! Please! Open up!'*

It was so dark, she couldn't even tell if her eyes were open. She pressed against the door, not wanting to take her hands away because it was her only point of reference in the pure dark. Take them away, turn around, and she would be spinning in an endless dark void.

Hadn't Mark and Daniel seen the body through the open door? Obviously not. But they must have heard her. She had screamed just before the door shut. Now they knew she was here, they would open it immediately! Wouldn't they?

they locked me in . . .

It took a second for the realization to sink in. Not *they shut me in*. Not *they accidentally closed the door on me*. Just *they locked me in* . . . and then, *i fink they all went home*.

'Oh no,' Juliet whispered. 'Mark and Daniel!' She sank down to the floor with her back against the cold metal door.

im scared
i cant get out
im freezin

Juliet didn't know how long passed before she started thinking in a straight line again. She had to get out, and it was obvious that Mark and Daniel weren't coming back for her. She had dropped her phone – well, she had to find it again. Juliet got on to her knees and crawled forward, moving her hands across the ceramic tiles in front of her. Every second she was braced for the moment that she might miss the phone and feel her fingers brush against Luke instead.

She felt her hand knock against something small and hard. It clattered across the floor, but she grabbed it before it could get too far. Then, by feel, she pressed the menu button.

The display and the keypad lit up in green, and she breathed a grateful sigh. She had light. She had a way of talking to the world.

im ya friend i need u

The damp, stinking air pressed around her. Juliet didn't know how much oxygen was in this steel crypt, but if she kept calm it should last a while. Long enough for someone to come and get her. She called up the messages menu, thumbed out the words *help me*, and selected Christine's number.

The whirling envelope appeared on screen, showing that the message was being sent. Juliet slumped back against the wall with relief.

The phone beeped and she smiled in the dark, then checked to see what Christine had said.

It wasn't from Christine, and though she stared at the screen for a long time, the words just wouldn't sink in.

Error — unable to send msg

When she finally figured it out, she knew without a trace of uncertainty that Luke had had the same thought one year ago, when his desperate messages failed to arrive. She was wrapped in a steel-lined coffin. No phone signal would get through this. Her mobile didn't have a chance.

Juliet screamed.

Terrify yourself with more books from Nick Shadow's
Midnight Library

Vol. I: *Voices*

Kate knows that something is wrong when she starts hearing voices in her head. But she doesn't know what the voices mean, or what terror they will lead her to . . .

Vol. II: *Blood and Sand*

John and Sarah are on the most boring seaside holiday of their lives. And when they come up against the sinister Sandman, they really begin to wish they'd stayed at home . . .

Vol. IV: *The Cat Lady*

Chloe never quite believed her friend's stories about the Cat Lady. But when a dare goes horribly wrong, she finds out tht the truth is more terrifying than anyone had ever imagined . . .